'Full of moving things and happenings . . . One of the most important
~~~~~~~~~~~~~~~~ A. S. B~~~~~~~~~~~~~~~~

'Overwhelmingly my Book of the Year. One of the finest literary
minds at work anywhere. Simply wonderful' Eileen Battersby,
Irish Times, Books of the Year

'Strange, mesmeric, sublimely beautiful . . . in parts a brilliant book'
Mail on Sunday

'A terrifying diving-bell descent into the drowned landscape of
European history, an underwater archaeology of lost time. Book of
the Year in any genre' *Time Out*

'One puts this wonderful novel down persuaded that Mr Sebald has
marshalled his literary strengths on a scale greater than any he
achieved before' *Washington Times*

'A profound meditation on tradition and time, suffused by a sense of
mortality and decay. Character and place are both richly imagined.
An exceptional novel' *Daily Mail*

'So convincing; spellbindingly accomplished; a work of art . . . a
wonderful book' *The Times Literary Supplement*

'A wonderful, dreamy, nostalgic account . . . Sebald has invented
a disturbing, inverted new take on ghosts, for whom we are the
unreal people. He is one of the most gripping writers imaginable'
New York Review

'W. G. Sebald's are some of the most original and exhilarating books
of our times' *Washington Post*

'History, landscape, memory, identity and exile . . . the story of *Austerlitz* is wrapped up in layer upon layer of exquisite poetic expositions. An extraordinary articulate dream' *The Times*

'Deadpan comedy, romantic scene-painting, mellifluous yet painstaking style . . . Sebald makes exquisite art out of vile history' Boyd Tonkin, *Independent*

'The most powerful fiction. I have never read a book that provides such a powerful account of the devastation wrought by the dispersal of the Jews from Prague and their treatment by the Nazis. A literary tour de force' *Observer*

'Haunting, challenging and intriguing . . . a strikingly rewarding read' *Metro*

'Sebald is unique. This is a great novel. It is already a classic' *Irish Independent*

'Sebald's best book yet' Geoff Dyer, *Independent on Sunday*

'Sebald writes about how grand events echo in the lives of individuals, and of the corrosive effects of time and memory' *Economist*

'Includes passages with the rawness of a rare, good memoir, and the momentum of – rarer still – a convincing historical epic' *Guardian*

'Childhood, displacement, loss, nostalgia and, above all, fear – the fear of history, of event, of human cruelty, of the pain of recollection – find their deepest and most brutal expression here. His art is a form of justice – there can be no higher aim' Rachel Cusk, *Evening Standard*

'Moving, rich, brilliant . . . Sebald [is] the most haunting of German writers' *The New York Times Review of Books*

'Compelling. So convincing that one is obliged to recognize the truly phenomenal configuration of the author's mind. *Austerlitz* [is] the most accomplished of Sebald's works' Anita Brookner, *Spectator*

ABOUT THE AUTHOR AND TRANSLATOR

W. G. Sebald was born in Wertach im Allgäu, Germany, in 1944. He studied German language and literature in Freiburg, Switzerland and Manchester. In 1966 he took up a position as an assistant lecturer at the University of Manchester, and settled permanently in England in 1970. He was Professor of European Literature at the University of East Anglia until his death in December 2001. He is the author of the long prose poem *After Nature* and three other works of fiction: *The Emigrants*, which won a series of major awards, including the Berlin Literature Prize, the Heinrich Böll Prize, the Heinrich Heine Prize and the Joseph Breitbach Prize; *The Rings of Saturn*; and *Vertigo*.

Anthea Bell was born in Suffolk and educated at Somerville College, Oxford. She has worked as a translator for many years, primarily from German and French. Her past translations include works of non-fiction, literary and popular fiction, and books for young people, among them classic German works by the Brothers Grimm, Clemens Brentano, Wilhelm Hauff and Christian Morgenstern. She has served three terms on the committee of the Translators' Association of the UK, and has received a number of translation prizes and awards.

Austerlitz

W.G. SEBALD

Translated from the German by Anthea Bell

PENGUIN BOOKS

PENGUIN BOOKS

Published by the Penguin Group
Penguin Books Ltd, 80 Strand, London wc2r orl, England
Penguin Putnam Inc., 375 Hudson Street, New York, New York 10014, USA
Penguin Books Australia Ltd, 250 Camberwell Road,
Camberwell, Victoria 3124, Australia
Penguin Books Canada Ltd, 10 Alcorn Avenue, Toronto, Ontario, Canada m4v 3b2
Penguin Books India (P) Ltd, 11 Community Centre,
Panchsheel Park, New Delhi – 110 017, India
Penguin Books (NZ) Ltd, Cnr Rosedale and Airborne Roads,
Albany, Auckland, New Zealand
Penguin Books (South Africa) (Pty) Ltd, 24 Sturdee Avenue,
Rosebank 2196, South Africa

Penguin Books Ltd, Registered Offices: 80 Strand, London wc2r orl, England

www.penguin.com

First published in German by Carl Hanser Verlag 2001
First published in Great Britain by Hamish Hamilton 2001
Published in Penguin Books 2002

1

Set in Monotype Perpetua
Printed in England by Clays Ltd, St Ives plc

at last, plagued by a headache and my uneasy thoughts, I took refuge in the zoo by the Astridplein, next to the Centraal Station, waiting for the pain to subside. I sat there on a bench in dappled shade, beside an aviary full of brightly feathered finches and siskins fluttering about. As the afternoon drew to a close I walked through the park, and finally went to see the Nocturama, which had first been opened only a few months earlier. It was some time before my eyes became used to its artificial dusk, and I could make out the different animals leading their sombrous lives behind the glass by the light of a pale moon. I cannot now recall exactly what creatures I saw on that visit to the Antwerp Nocturama, but there were probably bats and jerboas from Egypt and the Gobi Desert, native European hedgehogs and owls, Australian opossums, pine martens, dormice and lemurs, leaping from branch to branch, darting back and forth over the greyish-yellow sandy ground, or disappearing into a bamboo thicket. The only animal which has remained lingering in my memory is the racoon. I watched it for a long time as it sat beside a little stream with a serious expression on its face, washing the same piece of apple over and over again, as if it hoped that all this washing, which went far beyond any reasonable thoroughness, would help it to escape the unreal world in which it had arrived, so to speak, through no fault of its own. Otherwise, all I remember of the denizens of the Nocturama is that several of them had strikingly large eyes, and the fixed,

inquiring gaze found in certain painters and philosophers who seek to penetrate the darkness

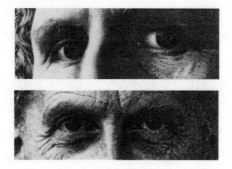

which surrounds us purely by means of looking and thinking. I believe that my mind also dwelt on the question of whether the electric light was turned on for the creatures in the Nocturama when real night fell and the zoo was closed to the public, so that as day dawned over their topsy-turvy miniature universe they could fall asleep with some degree of reassurance. Over the years, images of the interior of the Nocturama have become confused in my mind with my memories of the *Salle des pas perdus*, as it is called, in Antwerp Centraal Station. If I try to conjure up a picture of that waiting-room today I immediately see the Nocturama, and if I think of the Nocturama the waiting-room springs to my mind, probably because when I left the zoo that afternoon I went straight into the station, or rather first stood in the square outside it for some time to look up at the façade of that fantastical building, which I had taken in only vaguely when I arrived in the morning. Now, however, I saw how far the station constructed under the patronage of King Leopold II exceeded its purely utilitarian function, and I marvelled at the verdigris-covered negro boy who, for a century now, has sat upon his dromedary on top of an oriel turret to the left of the station façade, a monument to the world of the animals and native which had included a strikingly large number of dwarf species – tiny fennec foxes, springhares, hamsters – the railway passengers seemed to me somehow miniaturized, whether by the unusual height of the ceiling or because of the gathering dusk, and it was this, I suppose, which prompted the passing thought, nonsensical in itself, that they were the last members of a diminutive race which had perished or had been expelled from its homeland, and that because they alone survived they wore the same sorrowful expression as the creatures in the zoo. One of the people waiting in the *Salle des pas perdus* was Austerlitz, a man who then, in 1967, appeared almost youthful, with fair, curiously wavy hair of a kind I had seen elsewhere only on the German hero Siegfried in Fritz Lang's *Nibelungen* film. That day in Antwerp, as on all our later meetings, Austerlitz wore heavy walking boots and workman's trousers made of faded blue calico, together with a tailor-made but long outdated suit jacket. Apart from these externals he also differed from the other travellers in being the only one who was not staring apathetically into space, but instead was occupied in making notes and sketches obviously relating to the room where we were both sitting — a magnificent hall more suitable, to my mind, for a state ceremony than as a place to wait for the next connection to Paris or Oostende — for when he was not actually writing something down his glance often dwelt on the row of windows, the fluted pilasters, and other structural details of the waiting-room. Once Austerlitz took a camera out of his rucksack, an old Ensign with telescopic bellows, and took several pictures of the mirrors, which were now quite dark, but so far I have been unable to find them among the many hundreds of pictures, most of them unsorted, that he entrusted to me soon after we met again in the winter of 1996. When I finally went over to Austerlitz with a question about his obvious interest in the waiting-room, he was not at all surprised by my direct approach but answered me at once, without the slightest hesitation, as I have variously found since that solitary travellers, who so often pass days on end in uninterrupted silence, are glad to be spoken to. Now and then they are even ready to open up to a stranger unreservedly on such occasions, although that was not the case with Austerlitz in the *Salle des pas perdus*, nor did he subsequently tell me very much about his origins and his own life. Our Antwerp conversations, as he sometimes called them later, turned primarily on architectural history, in accordance with his own astonishing professional expertise, and it was the subject we discussed that evening as we sat together until nearly midnight in the restaurant facing the waiting-room on the other side of the great domed hall. The few guests still lingering at that late hour one by one deserted the buffet, which was constructed like a mirror image of the waiting-room, until we were left alone with a solitary man drinking Fernet and the barmaid, who sat enthroned on a stool behind the counter, legs crossed, filing her nails with complete devotion and concentration. Austerlitz commented in passing of this lady, whose peroxide-blonde hair was piled up into a sort of bird's nest, that she was the goddess of time past. And on the wall behind her, under the lion crest of the kingdom of Belgium, there was indeed a mighty clock, the dominating feature of the buffet, with a hand some six feet long travelling round a dial which had once been gilded, but was now blackened by railway soot and tobacco smoke. During the pauses in our conversation we both noticed what an endless length of time went by before another minute had passed, and how alarming seemed the movement of that hand, which resembled a sword of justice, even though we were expecting it every time it jerked forward, slicing off the next one-sixtieth of an hour from the future and coming to a halt with such a menacing quiver that one's heart almost stopped. Towards the end of the nineteenth century, Austerlitz began, in reply to my questions about the history of the building of Antwerp station, when Belgium, a little patch of yellowish grey barely visible on the map of the world, spread its sphere of influence to the African continent with its colonial enterprises, when deals of huge proportions were done on the capital markets and raw-materials exchanges of Brussels, and the citizens of Belgium, full of boundless optimism, believed that their country, which had been subject so long to foreign rule and was divided and disunited in itself, was about to become a great new economic power – at that time, now so long ago although it determines our lives to this day, it was the personal wish of King Leopold, under whose auspices such apparently inexorable progress was being made, that the money suddenly and abundantly available should be used to erect public buildings which would bring international renown to his aspiring state. One of the projects thus initiated by the highest authority in the land was the central station of the Flemish metropolis where we were sitting now, said Austerlitz; designed by Louis Delacenserie, it was inaugurated in the summer of 1905, after ten years of planning and building, in the presence of the King himself. The model Leopold had recommended to his architects was the new railway station of Lucerne, where he had been particularly struck by the concept of the dome, so dramatically exceeding the usual modest height of railway buildings,* a concept realized by Delacenserie in his own design, which was inspired by the Pantheon in Rome, in such

* On looking through these notes I remember that in February 1971, during a short visit to Switzerland, one of the places I visited was Lucerne. After seeing the Glacier Museum I spent some time standing on the bridge over the lake on my way back to the station, because the view of its dome and the snow-white heights of the Pilatus massif rising in the clear winter sky behind it had reminded me of my conversation with Austerlitz in Antwerp four and a half years earlier. A few hours later, on the night of 4 February, long after I was fast asleep in my hotel room in Zurich,

a fire broke out in Lucerne Station, spread very rapidly and entirely destroyed the domed building. I could not get the pictures I saw next day in the newspapers and on television out of my head for several weeks, and they gave me an uneasy, anxious feeling which crystallized into the idea that I had been

stupendous fashion that even today, said Austerlitz, exactly as the architect intended, when we
step into the entrance hall we are seized by a
sense of being beyond the profane, in a cathedral
consecrated to international traffic and trade.
Delacenserie borrowed the main elements of his
monumental structure from the palaces of the
Italian Renaissance, but he also struck Byzantine
and Moorish notes, and perhaps when I arrived,
said Austerlitz, I myself had noticed the round grey
and white granite turrets, the sole purpose of
which was to arouse medieval associations in the
minds of railway passengers. However laughable
in itself, Delacenserie's eclecticism, uniting past
and future in the Centraal Station with its marble
stairway in the foyer and the steel and glass roof
spanning the platforms, was in fact a logical stylistic approach to the new epoch, said Austerlitz,
and it was also appropriate, he continued, that
in Antwerp Station the elevated level from which
the gods looked down on visitors to the Roman

to blame, or at least one of those to blame, for the Lucerne
fire. In my dreams, even years later, I sometimes saw the
flames leaping from the dome and lighting up the entire
panorama of the snow-covered Alps.

obliged to adjust their activities to its demands. In fact, said Austerlitz, until the railway timetables were synchronized the clocks of Lille and Liège did not keep the same time as the clocks of Ghent and Antwerp, and not until they were all standardized around the middle of the nineteenth century did time truly reign supreme. It was only by following the course time prescribed that we could hasten through the gigantic spaces separating us from each other. And indeed, said Austerlitz after a while, to this day there is something illusionistic and illusory about the relationship of time and space as we experience it in travelling, which is why whenever we come home from elsewhere we never feel quite sure if we have really been abroad. From the first I was astonished by the way Austerlitz put his ideas together as he talked, forming perfectly balanced sentences out of whatever occurred to him, so to speak, and the way in which, in his mind, the passing on of his knowledge seemed to become a gradual approach to a kind of historical metaphysic, bringing remembered events back to life. I shall never forget how he concluded his comments on the manufacture of the tall waiting-room mirrors by wondering, glancing up once more at canary-yellow dress, and the cavalier bending over her in concern is clad in red breeches, very conspicuous in the pallid light. Looking at the river now, thinking of that painting and its tiny figures, said Austerlitz, I feel as if the moment depicted by Lucas van Valckenborch had never come to an end, as if the canary-yellow lady had only just fallen over or swooned, as if the black velvet hood had only this moment dropped away from her head, as if the little accident, which no doubt goes unnoticed by most viewers, were always happening over and over again, and nothing and no one could ever remedy it. On that day, after we had left our viewing point on the promenade to stroll through the inner city, Austerlitz spoke at length about the marks of pain which, as he said he well knew, trace countless fine lines through history. In his studies of railway architecture, he said when we were sitting in a bistro in the Glove Market later that afternoon, tired from our wandering through the city, he could never quite shake off thoughts of the agony of leave-taking and the fear of foreign places, although such ideas were not part of architectural history proper. Yet, he said, it is often our mightiest projects that most obviously betray the degree of our insecurity. The construction of fortifications, for instance – and Antwerp was an outstanding example of that craft – clearly showed how we feel obliged to keep surrounding ourselves with defences, built in successive phases as a precaution against any incursion by enemy powers, until the idea of concentric rings making their way steadily outward comes up against its natural limits. If we study the development of fortifications from Floriani, da Capri and San Micheli, by way of Rusenstein, Burgsdorff, Coehoorn and Klengel, and so to Vauban and Montalembert, it is amazing, said Austerlitz, to see the persistence with which generations of masters of the art of military architecture, for all their undoubtedly outstanding gifts, clung to what we can easily see today was a fundamentally wrong-headed idea: the notion that by designing an ideal tracé with blunt bastions and ravelins projecting well beyond it, allowing the cannon of the fortress to cover the entire operational area outside the walls, you could make a city as secure as anything in the world can ever be. No one today, said Austerlitz, has the faintest idea of the boundless amount of theoretical writings on the building of fortifications, of the fantastic nature of the geometric, trigonometric and logistical calculations they record, of the inflated excesses of the professional vocabulary of fortification and siegecraft, no one now understands its simplest terms, *escarpe* and *courtine*, *faussebraie*, *réduit* and *glacis*, yet even from our present standpoint we can see that towards the end of the seventeenth century the star-shaped dodecagon behind

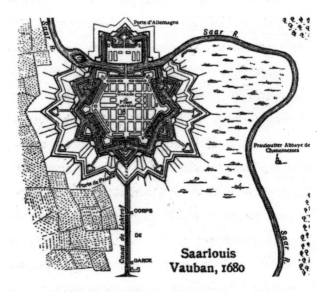

Saarlouis
Vauban, 1680

trenches had finally crystallized, out of the various available systems, as the preferred ground-plan: a kind of ideal typical pattern derived from the

Golden Section, which indeed, as study of the intricately sketched plans of such fortified complexes as those of Coevorden, Neuf-Brisach and Saarlouis will show, immediately strikes the layman as an emblem both of absolute power and of the ingenuity the engineers put to the service of that power. In the practice of warfare, however, the star-shaped fortresses which were being built and improved everywhere during the eighteenth century did not answer their purpose, for intent as everyone was on that pattern, it had been forgotten that the largest fortifications will naturally attract the largest enemy forces, and that the more you entrench yourself the more you must remain on the defensive, so that in the end you might find yourself in a place fortified in every possible way, watching helplessly while the enemy troops, moving on to their own choice of terrain elsewhere, simply ignored their adversaries' fortresses, which had become positive arsenals of weaponry, bristling with cannon and overcrowded with men. The frequent result, said Austerlitz, of resorting to measures of fortification marked in general by a tendency towards paranoid elaboration was that you drew attention to your weakest the construction of a new *enceinte* ten miles long, with eight forts situated over half an hour's march away from it, a project which proved inadequate after less than twenty years because of the longer range of modern guns and the increasingly destructive power of explosives, so that, in obedience to the same old logic, construction now began on yet another ring of fifteen heavily fortified outworks six to nine miles away from the *enceinte*. During the thirty years or more it took to build this complex the question arose, as was only to be expected, said Austerlitz, of whether the expansion of Antwerp beyond the old city boundaries through its rapid industrial and commercial development did not mean that the line of forts ought to be moved yet another three miles further out, which would actually have made it over thirty miles long, bringing it within sight of the outskirts of Mechelen, with the result that the entire Belgian army would have been insufficient to garrison the fortifications. So, said Austerlitz, they just went on working to complete the system already under construction, although they knew it was now far from being able to meet the actual requirements. The last link in the chain was the fortress of

Breendonk, said Austerlitz, a fort completed just before the outbreak of the First World War in which, within a few months, it proved completely useless for the defence of the city and the country. Such complexes of fortifications, said Austerlitz, concluding his remarks that day in the Antwerp Glove Market as he rose from the table and slung his rucksack over his shoulder, show us how, unlike birds, for instance, who keep building the same nest over thousands of years, we tend to forge ahead with our projects far beyond any reasonable bounds. Someone, he added, ought to draw up a catalogue of types of buildings, listed in order of size, and it would be immediately obvious that domestic buildings of *less* than normal size — the little cottage in the fields, the hermitage, the lock-keeper's lodge, the pavilion for viewing the landscape, the children's bothy in the garden — are those that offer us at least a semblance of peace, whereas no one in his right mind could truthfully say that he liked a vast edifice such as the Palace of Justice on the old Gallows Hill in Brussels. At the most we gaze at it in wonder, a kind of wonder which in itself is a form of dawning horror, for somehow we know by instinct that outsize short distance to Mechelen, where a bus runs from outside the station to the small town of Willebroek; it is on the outskirts of this town that the fort stands in its grounds of some ten hectares, set among the fields rather like an island in the sea and surrounded by an embankment, a barbed-wire fence and a wide moat. It was unusually hot for the time of year, and large cumulus clouds were piling up on the south-west horizon as I crossed the bridge over the dark water. After the previous day's conversation, I still had an image in my head of a star-shaped bastion with walls towering above a precise geometrical ground-plan, but what I now saw before me was a low-built concrete mass, rounded at all its outer edges and giving the gruesome impression of something hunched and misshapen: the broad back of a monster, I thought, risen from this Flemish soil like a whale from the deep. I felt reluctant to pass through the black gateway into the fortress itself, and instead began by walking round it on the outside, through the unnaturally deep green, almost blue-tinged grass growing on the island. From whatever viewpoint I tried to form a picture of the complex I could make out no architectural plan, for its projections and indentations kept shifting, so far exceeding my comprehension that in the end I found myself unable to connect it with anything shaped by human civilization, or even with the silent relics of our prehistory and early history. And the longer I

looked at it, the more often it forced me, as I felt, to lower my eyes, the less comprehensible it seemed to become. Covered in places by open ulcers with the raw crushed stone erupting from them, encrusted by guano-like droppings and calcareous streaks, the fort was a monolithic, monstrous incarnation of ugliness and blind violence. Even later, when I studied the symmetrical ground-plan with its outgrowths of limbs and

claws, with the semi-circular bastions standing out from the front of the main building like eyes, and the stumpy projection at the back of its body, I could not, despite its now evident rational structure, recognize anything designed by the human

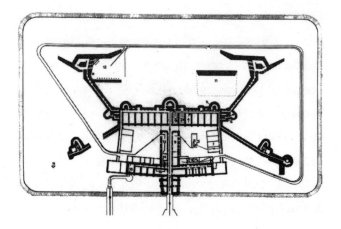

mind but saw it, rather, as the anatomical blue-print of some alien and crab-like creature. The path round the fort led past the tarred black posts of the execution ground, and the labour site where the prisoners had to clear away the earth-works around the walls, moving over a quarter of a million tons of soil and rubble with only shovels and wheelbarrows to help them. These wheel-barrows, one of which can still be seen in the anteroom of the fort, must have seemed terrify-ingly primitive even then. They consisted of a kind of stretcher with two crude handles at one end and an iron-shod wooden wheel at the other. A container with sloping sides, roughly cobbled together from unplaned planks, stood on the crossbars of the stretcher, the whole clumsy con-traption resembling the handcarts used by farmers where I lived as a child for clearing muck out of the stables, except that the wheelbarrows in Breendonk were twice as large, and even when they were empty must have reached around a hundredweight. I could not imagine how the prisoners, very few of whom had probably ever done hard physical labour before their arrest and internment, could have pushed these barrows full of heavy detritus over the sun-baked clay of the ground, furrowed by ruts as hard as stone, or through the mire that was churned up after a single day's rain; it was impossible to picture them bracing themselves against the weight until their hearts nearly burst, or think of the overseer beating them about the head with the handle of a shovel when they could not move forward. However, if I could not envisage the drudgery performed day after day, year after year, at Breendonk and all the other main and branch camps, when I finally entered the fort itself and glanced through the glass panes of a door on the right into the so-called mess of the SS guards with its scrubbed tables and benches, its bulging stove and the various adages neatly painted on its wall in Gothic lettering, I could well imagine the sight of the good fathers and dutiful sons from Vilsbiburg and Fuhlsbüttel, from the Black Forest and the Bavarian Alps, sitting here when they came off duty to play cards or write letters to their loved ones at home. After all, I had lived among them until my twentieth year. My memory of the fourteen stations which the visitor to Breendonk passes between the entrance and the exit has clouded over in the course of time, or perhaps I could say it was clouding over even on the day when I was in the fort, whether because I did not really want to see what it had to show or because all the outlines seemed to merge in a world illuminated only by a few dim electric bulbs, and cut

off for ever from the light of nature. Even now, when I try to remember them, when I look back at the crab-like plan of Breendonk and read the words of the captions – *Former Office*, *Printing Works*, *Huts*, *Jacques Ochs Hall*, *Solitary Confinement Cell*, *Mortuary*, *Relics Store* and *Museum* – the darkness does not lift but becomes yet heavier as I think how little we can hold in mind, how everything is constantly lapsing into oblivion with every extinguished life, how the world is, as it were, draining itself, in that the history of countless places and objects which themselves have no power of memory is never heard, never described or passed on. Histories, for instance, like those of the straw mattresses which lay, shadow-like, on the stacked plank beds and which had become thinner and shorter because the chaff in them disintegrated over the years, shrunken – and now, in writing this, I do remember that such a idea occurred to me at the time – as if they were the mortal frames of those who once lay there in that darkness. I also recollect now that as I went on down the tunnel which could be said to form the backbone of the fort, I had to resist the feeling taking root in my heart, one which to this day often comes over me in macabre places, a sense that with every forward step the air was growing thinner and the weight above me heavier. At the time, anyway, in that silent noonday hour in the early summer of 1967 which I spent inside the fort of Breendonk, encountering no other visitors, I hardly dared to go on to the point where, at the end of a second long tunnel, a corridor not much more than the height of a man, and (as I think I remember) somewhat sloping, leads down to one of the casemates. This casemate, in which you sense immediately that there

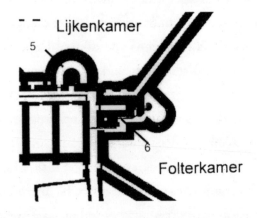

is a layer of concrete several metres thick overhead, is a narrow room with walls converging at a sharp angle on one side, rounded on the other, and with its floor at least a foot lower than the passage giving access to it, so that it is less like an oubliette than a pit. As I stared at the smooth, grey floor of this pit, which seemed to me to be sinking further and further down, the grating over the drain in the middle of it and the metal pail standing beside the drain, a picture of our laundry room at home in W. rose from the abyss and with it, suggested perhaps by the iron hook hanging on a cord from the ceiling, the image of the butcher's shop I always had to pass on my way to school, where at noon Benedikt was often to be seen in a rubber apron washing down the tiles with a thick hose. No one can explain exactly what happens within us when the doors behind which our childhood terrors lurk are flung open. But I do remember that there in the casemate at Breendonk a nauseating smell of soft soap rose to my nostrils, and that this smell, in some strange place in my head, was linked to the bizarre German word for scrubbing-brush, *Wurzelbürste*, which was a favourite of my father's and which I had always disliked. Black striations began to quiver before my eyes, and I had to rest my forehead against the wall, which was gritty, covered with bluish spots, and seemed to me to be perspiring with cold beads of sweat. It was not that as the nausea rose in me I guessed at the kind of third-degree interrogations which were being conducted here around the time I was born, since it was only a few years later that I read Jean Améry's description of the dreadful physical closeness between torturers and their victims, and that after his liberation from the camp he found the sight of a German, or indeed any so-called civilized being, male or female, so intolerable that, hardly recovered, he embarked on the first ship he could find, to make his living prospecting for diamonds and gold in South America. For some time Novelli lived in the green jungle with a tribe of small people who had gleaming, coppery skins and had emerged beside him as if out of nowhere one day, without moving so much as a leaf. He adopted their customs, and to the best of his ability compiled a dictionary of their language, consisting almost entirely of vowels, particularly the sound A in countless variations of intonation and emphasis, not a word of which, Simon writes, had yet been recorded by the Linguistic Institute in São Paulo. Later Novelli returned to his native land and began to paint pictures. His main subject, depicted again and again in different forms and compositions — *filiforme, gras, soudain plus épais ou plus grand, puis de nouveau mince, boiteux* — was the letter A, which he traced on the coloured ground he had applied sometimes with the point of a pencil, sometimes with the stem of his brush or an even blunter instrument, in ranks of scarcely legible ciphers crowding closely together and above one another, always the same and yet never repeating themselves, rising and falling in waves like a long-drawn-out scream.

AAAAAAAAAAAAAAAAAAAAAAAAAAAAAAAAA
AAAAAAAAAAAAAAAAAAAAAAAAAAAAAAAAA
AAAAAAAAAAAAAAAAAAAAAAAAAAAAAAAAA

Although Austerlitz did not reappear in the Glove Market in Antwerp that June day in 1967 on which, in the end, I went out to Breendonk, our paths kept crossing, in a way that I still find hard to understand, on all my Belgian excursions of that time, none of them planned in advance. A few days after our first encounter in the *Salle des pas perdus* of the Centraal Station, I met him again in an industrial quarter on the south-western out-skirts of the city of Liège, which I had reached towards evening, coming on foot from St Georges-sur-Meuse and Flémalle. The sun was just breaking once again through the inky blue wall of cloud heralding a storm, and the factory buildings and yards, the long rows of terraced housing for the labourers, the brick walls, the slate roofs and the window panes shone as if a fire were glowing within them. When the rain began lashing down on the streets I took refuge in a tiny bar called, as I remember, the Café des Espérances, where to my considerable surprise I found Austerlitz bent over his notes at one of the Formica tables. On this second meeting, as on all subsequent occasions, we simply went on with our conversation, wasting no time in commenting on the improbability of our meeting again in a place like this, which no sensible person would have sought out. From where we sat until late that evening in the Café des Espérances, you could look through a back window down into a valley, perhaps a place of water meadows in the past, where now the reflected light from the blast furnaces of a gigantic iron foundry glared against the dark sky, and I remember clearly how, as we both gazed intently at this spectacle, Austerlitz launched into a discourse of over two hours on the way in which, during the nineteenth century, the vision of model towns for workers entertained by philanthropic entrepreneurs had inadvertently changed into the practice of accommodating them in barracks — just as our best-laid plans, said Austerlitz, as I still remember, always turn into

the exact opposite when they are put into practice. It was several months after this meeting in
Liège that I came upon Austerlitz, again entirely
by chance, on the old Gallows Hill in Brussels, on
the steps of the Palace of Justice which, as he
immediately told me, is the largest accumulation
of stone blocks anywhere in Europe. The building
of this singular architectural monstrosity, on
which Austerlitz was planning to write a study at
the time, began in the 1880s at the urging of the

bourgeoisie of Brussels, over-hastily and before the details of the grandiose scheme submitted by a certain Joseph Poelaert had been properly worked out, as a result of which, said Austerlitz, this huge pile of over seven hundred thousand cubic metres contains corridors and stairways leading nowhere, and doorless rooms and halls where no one would ever set foot, empty spaces surrounded by walls and representing the innermost secret of all sanctioned authority. Austerlitz went on to tell me that he himself, looking for a labyrinth used in the initiation ceremonies of the freemasons, which he had heard was in either the basement or the attic storey of the palace, had wandered for hours through this mountain range of stone, through forests of columns, past colossal statues, upstairs and downstairs, and no one ever asked him what he wanted. During these wanderings, feeling tired or wishing to get his bearings from the sky, he had stopped at one of the windows set deep in the walls to look out over the leaden grey roofs of the palace, crammed together like pack ice, and down into ravines and shaft-like interior courtyards never penetrated by any ray of light. He had gone on and on down the corridors, said

I heard several such apocryphal stories from Austerlitz, anecdotes in curious contrast to his usual rigorous objectivity, not only that day but on our later encounters, for instance one quiet November afternoon when we spent some time sitting in a café with a billiards room in Terneuzen – I still remember the proprietress, a woman with thick-lensed spectacles who was knitting a grass-green sock, the glowing nuggets of coke in the hearth, the damp sawdust on the floor, the bitter smell of chicory – and looked out through the panoramic window, which was framed by the tentacles of an ancient rubber plant, at the vast expanse of the misty grey mouth of the Schelde. Then, not long before Christmas, I saw Auster-litz coming towards me on the promenade at Zeebrugge when evening was falling and there was not another living soul in sight. It turned out that we had both booked on the same ferry, so we slowly walked back to the harbour together, with the emptiness of the North Sea on our right and on our right the tall façades of the apartment blocks set among the dunes, with the bluish light of tele-vision screens flickering behind their windows, curiously unsteady and ghostly. It was night by the

Almost every time I went to London in the years that followed I visited Austerlitz where he worked in Bloomsbury, not far from the British Museum. I would usually spend an hour or so sitting with him in his crowded study, which was like a stock-room of books and papers with hardly any space left for himself, let alone his students, among the

stacks piled high on the floor and the overloaded shelves. When I began my own studies in Germany I had learnt almost nothing from the scholars then lecturing in the humanities there, most of them academics who had built their careers in the 1930s and 1940s and still nurtured delusions of power, and I found Austerlitz the first teacher I could listen to since my time in primary school. I remember to this day how easily I could grasp what he called his tentative ideas when he talked about the architectural style of the capitalist era, a subject which he said had fascinated him since his own student days, speaking in particular of the compulsive sense of order and the tendency towards monumentalism evident in lawcourts and penal institutions, railway stations and stock exchanges, opera houses and lunatic asylums, and the dwellings built to rectangular grid patterns for the labour force. His investigations, so Austerlitz once told me, had long outstripped their original purpose as a project for a dissertation, proliferating in his hands into endless preliminary sketches for a study, based entirely on his own views, of the family likeness between all these buildings. Why he had embarked on such a wide field, said Austerlitz, he did not know; very likely he had been poorly advised when he first began his research work. But then again, it was also true that he was still obeying an impulse which he himself, to this day, did not really understand, but which was somehow linked to his early fascination with the idea of a network far as I remember I wrote to Austerlitz from Munich a couple of times, but I never had any reply to my letters, either because, as I thought at the time, Austerlitz was away somewhere, or as I now think because he did not like writing to Germany. Whatever the reason for his silence, the link between us was broken, and I did not renew it when, scarcely a year later, I decided to return to the United Kingdom. It would now of course have been up to me to let Austerlitz know of the unforeseen change to my plans, and my failure to do so may have resulted from the fact that soon after my return I went through a difficult period which dulled my sense of other people's existence, and from which I only very gradually emerged by turning back to the writing I had long neglected. At any rate, I did not often think of Austerlitz in all those years, and when the thought of him did cross my mind I always forgot him again next moment, so that we did not in fact resume our old relationship, which had been both a close and a distant one, until two decades later in December 1996, and through a curious chain of circumstances. I was in some anxiety at the time because I had noticed, looking up an address in the telephone book, that the sight in my right eye had almost entirely disappeared overnight, so to speak. Even when I glanced up from the page open in front of me and turned my gaze on the framed photographs on the wall, all my right eye could see was a row of dark shapes curiously distorted above and below – the figures and landscapes familiar to me in every detail having resolved indiscriminately into a black and menacing cross-hatching. At the same time I kept feeling as if I could see as clearly as ever on the edge of my field of vision, and had only to look sideways to rid myself of what I took at first for a merely hysterical weakness in my eyesight. Although I tried several times, I did not succeed. Instead, the grey areas seemed to be spreading, and now and then, opening and closing my eyes alternately to compare their degrees of clarity, I thought that I had suffered some impairment on the left as well. Considerably alarmed by what I feared was the progressive decline of my eyesight, I remembered reading once that until well into the nineteenth century a few drops of liquid distilled from belladonna, a plant of the nightshade family, used to be applied to the retinas of operatic divas before they went on stage, and those of young women about to be introduced to a suitor, with the result that their eyes shone with a rapt and almost supernatural radiance, but they themselves could see almost nothing. I no longer know how I connected this memory with my own condition that dark December morning, except that in my mind it had something to do with the deceptiveness of that star-like, beautiful gleam and the danger of its premature extinction, an idea which filled me with concern for my ability to continue working and at the same time, if I may so put it, with a vision of release in which I saw myself, free of the constant compulsion to read and write, sitting in a wicker chair in a garden, surrounded by a world of indistinct shapes recognizable only by their faint colours. Since there was no improvement in my condition over the next few days, I went to London just before Christmas to see a Czech ophthalmologist who had been recommended to me. As usual when I go down to London on my own, a kind of dull despair stirred within me on that December morning. I looked out at the flat, almost treeless landscape, the vast brown expanse of the ploughed fields, the railway

columbarium. It was around three in the afternoon by the time I reached Harley Street and one
of its mauve brick buildings, almost all of them
occupied by dermatologists, urologists, gynae-
cologists, neurologists, psychiatrists, ear, nose
and throat specialists and eye surgeons, and was
standing by the window in the soft lamplight of
Zdeněk Gregor's slightly over-heated waiting-
room. From the grey sky that lowered over the
city outside a few isolated snowflakes were floating down, and disappeared into the dark chasms
of the yards behind the buildings. I thought of the
onset of winter in the mountains, the complete
absence of sound, and my childhood wish for
everything to be snowed over, the whole village
and the valley all the way to the mountain peaks,
and how I used to imagine what it would be like
when we thawed out again and emerged from the
ice in spring. And as I stood in the waiting-room
remembering the snow of the Alps, the whitened
panes of the bedroom window, the curved drifts
around the porch, the softly capped insulators of
the telegraph poles, and the trough of the well
which was sometimes frozen over for months, the
opening lines of one of my favourite poems came

time reading and writing. After the consultation I must have a procedure called a fluorescing angiography carried out to determine the affected area of the retina more precisely – this would mean taking a series of photographs of my eyes or rather, if I understood him correctly, of the back of the eye through the iris, the pupil and the vitreous humour. The technician already waiting for me in a small room specially equipped for such purposes was a man of extraordinarily distinguished appearance who wore a white turban and looked, I foolishly thought, rather like the Prophet Muhammad. He carefully rolled up my shirt-sleeve, and inserted the tip of the needle into the prominent vein below the crook of my elbow without my feeling anything at all. While he was introducing the contrast medium into my bloodstream he said I might feel slightly unwell in a little while, and in any case my skin would be discoloured yellow for a few hours. After we had sat in silence for a moment or two, both in our respective places in the little room which, like a sleeping-car, was illuminated only by a dim bulb, he asked me to move closer to him and place my head in the framework fixed in a kind of stand on the table, with my chin in a shallow depression and my forehead against the iron band above it. As I write this I once again see the little points of light that shot into my widely opened eyes each time he pressed the shutter release. Half an hour later I was sitting in the saloon bar of the Great Eastern Hotel at Liverpool Street, waiting for the next train home. I had sought out a dark corner, since by now I did indeed feel rather qualmish inside my yellow skin. On the way to the station in the taxi we had seemed to be driving in a wide, looping trajectory through some kind of Luna Park, so strangely did the city lights turn beyond the windscreen, and now the dim globes of the sconces, the mirrors behind the bar and the colourful batteries of bottles of spirits were circling before my eyes as if I were on a roundabout. Leaning my head against the wall, and breathing deeply and slowly from time to time when I felt nausea rising, I had for a good while been watching the toilers in the City gold-mines as they came to meet at their usual watering hole early in the evening, all of them identical in their dark-blue suits, striped shirts and gaudy ties, and as I tried to grasp the mysterious habits of the members of this

his personal similarity to Ludwig Wittgenstein, and the horror-stricken expressions on both their faces. I believe it was mainly the rucksack, which Austerlitz told me later he had bought for ten shillings from Swedish stock in an army surplus store in the Charing Cross Road just before he began his studies, describing it as the only truly reliable thing in his life, which put into my head what on the surface was the rather outlandish idea

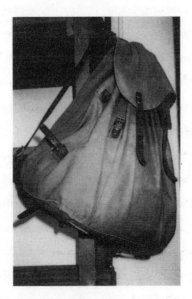

of a certain physical likeness between him and the philosopher who died of the disease of cancer in Cambridge in 1951. Wittgenstein always carried a rucksack too, in Puchberg and in Otterthal, when he went to Norway, Ireland, or Kazakhstan, or home to his sisters to spend Christmas with them in the Alleegasse. That rucksack, which his sister Margarete once told him in a letter was almost as dear to her as himself, went everywhere with him, even, I believe, across the Atlantic on the liner *Queen Mary*, and then on from New York to Ithaca. And now, whenever I see a photograph of Wittgenstein somewhere or other, I feel more and more as if Austerlitz were gazing at me out of it, and when I look at Austerlitz it is as if I see in him the disconsolate philosopher, a man locked into the glaring clarity of his logical thinking as inextricably as into his confused emotions, so striking is the likeness between the two of them: in stature, in the way they study one as if across an invisible barrier, in the makeshift organization of their lives, in a wish to manage with as few possessions as possible, and in the inability, typical of Austerlitz as it was of Wittgenstein, to linger over any kind of preliminaries. Accordingly, and without wasting any words on the coincidence of our meeting again after all this time, Austerlitz took up the conversation that evening in the bar of the

Great Eastern Hotel more or less where it had last been broken off. He had spent the afternoon, he told me, looking round the Great Eastern, which was soon to be thoroughly renovated, concentrating mainly on the freemasons' temple incorporated into the hotel by the directors of the railway company at the turn of the century, when the building had only just been completed and furnished with the utmost luxury. Though I really gave up my architectural studies long ago, he said, I sometimes relapse into my old habits, even if I don't make notes and sketches any more, but simply marvel at the strange edifices we construct. That had been the case today, when his way led him past the Great Eastern and, obeying a sudden impulse, he had gone into the foyer where, as it turned out, he had been very courteously received by the business manager, a Portuguese called Pereira, despite my request, said Austerlitz, which can't be one he hears every day, and despite my odd appearance. Pereira, Austerlitz went on, took me up a broad staircase to the first floor, produced a large key and unlocked the portal of the temple, a hall with walls panelled in sand-coloured marble and red Moroccan onyx, a black and white chequered floor, and a vaulted ceiling with a single golden star at the centre emitting its rays into the dark clouds all around it. Then Pereira and I went all over the hotel, most of it taken out of use already, through the great dining hall which could accommodate more than three hundred guests under its high glass dome,

through the smoking rooms and the billiards saloons, through suites and up staircases to the fourth floor where the kitchens used to be, and then down to the basement and the floor below the basement, once upon a time a cool labyrinth for the storage of Rhine wines, claret and champagne, for the making of thousands of items of pâtisserie and the preparation of vegetables, red meat and pale poultry. As for the fish section, where perch, pike, plaice, sole and eels lay heaped on black slate slabs with fresh water constantly running over them, Pereira described it as a whole underworld in itself, said Austerlitz, and if it hadn't been too late he, Austerlitz, would go round the place again with me. He added that he would particularly like to show me the temple, with its ornamental gold-painted picture of a three-storey ark floating beneath a rainbow, and the dove just returning to it carrying the olive branch in her beak. Oddly enough, said

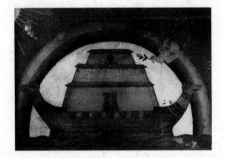

Austerlitz, as he stood in front of this attractive motif with Pereira that afternoon he had been

thinking of our encounters in Belgium, so long ago now, and telling himself he must find someone to whom he could relate his own story, a story which he had learned only in the last few years and for which he needed the kind of listener I had once been in Antwerp, Liège and Zeebrugge. Contrary to all statistical probability, then, there was an astonishing, positively imperative internal logic to his meeting me here in the bar of the Great Eastern Hotel, a place he had never before entered in his life. Having said this, Austerlitz fell silent, and for a while, it seemed to me, he gazed into the farthest distance. Since my childhood and youth, he finally began, looking at me again, I have never known who I really was. From where I stand now, of course, I can see that my name alone, and the fact that it was kept from me until my fifteenth year, ought to have put me on the track of my origins, but it has also become clear to me of late why an agency greater than or superior to my own capacity for thought, which circumspectly directs operations somewhere in my brain, has always preserved me from my own secret, systematically preventing me from drawing the obvious conclusions and embarking on the clothes had disappeared, to have to go around dressed in the English fashion in shorts, knee-length socks which were always slipping down, a string vest like a fish-net and a mouse-grey shirt, much too thin. I know that I often lay awake for hours in my narrow bed in the manse, trying to conjure up the faces of those whom I had left, I feared through my own fault, but not until I was numb with weariness and my eyelids sank in the darkness did I see my mother bending down to me just for a fleeting moment, or my father smiling as he put on his hat. Such comfort made it all the worse to wake up early in the morning and have to face the knowledge, new every day, that I was not at home now but very far away, in some kind of captivity. Only recently have I recalled how oppressed I felt, in all the time I spent with the Eliases, by the fact that they never opened a window, and perhaps that is why when I was out and about somewhere on a summer's day years later, and passed a house with all its windows thrown open, I felt an extraordinary sense of being carried away and out of myself. It was only a few days ago that, thinking over that experience of liberation, I remembered how one of the two said it was nothing, she had only caught a cold, and as she went out she ran her fingers through my hair, the one time, as far as I remember, she ever did such a thing. Meanwhile it was the minister's unalterable custom to sit in his study, which had a view of a dark corner of the garden, thinking about next Sunday's sermon. He never wrote any of these sermons down, but worked them out in his head, toiling over them for at least four days. He would always emerge from his study in the evening in a state of deep despondency, only to disappear into it again next morning. But on Sunday, when he stood up in chapel in front of his congregation and often addressed them for a full hour, he was a changed man; he spoke with a moving eloquence which I still feel I can hear, conjuring up before the eyes of his flock the Last Judgment awaiting them all, the lurid fires of purgatory, the torments of damnation and then, with the most wonderful stellar and celestial imagery, the entry of the righteous into eternal bliss. With apparent ease, as if he were making up the most appalling horrors as he went along, he always succeeded in filling the hearts of his congregation with such sentiments of remorse that at thin solid-ink pencil from the back of the book, moistening its tip with his tongue, and very slowly and neatly, like a schoolboy under supervision, noting down the name of the chapel where he had preached that day and the biblical passage he had taken as his text, for instance, under 20 July 1939: The Tabernacle, Llandrillo – *Psalms* CLXVII, 4, 'He telleth the number of the stars: he calleth them all by their names'; under 3 August 1941: Chapel Uchaf, Gilboa – *Zephaniah* III, 6, 'I have cut off the nations: their towers are desolate; I made their streets waste, that none passeth by'; and under 21 May 1944: Chapel Bethesda, Corwen – *Isaiah* XLVIII,18, 'O that thou hadst hearkened to my commandments! then had thy peace been as a river and thy righteousness as the waves of the sea!' The last entry in this little book, which is among those few of the minister's possessions to have passed into my hands after his death and through which I have often glanced recently, said Austerlitz, was made on one of the additional leaves inserted at the end and is dated 7 March 1952. It runs: Bala Chapel – *Psalms* CII, 6, 'I am like a pelican of the wilderness: I am like an owl of the desert.' For the most part, of course, now and then. And these light and dark sides of the minister Elias were reflected in the mountainous landscape around us. I remember, said Austerlitz, how we were once driving through the endless Tanat valley, with nothing on the hillsides to right and left of us but crooked bushes, ferns and rusty-hued vegetation, and then, for the last part of the way up to the col, only grey rock and drifting mist, so that I was afraid we were coming to the very ends of the earth. But on another day, when we had just reached the Pennant pass I saw a gap open up in the banked clouds towering high in the west, and the rays of the sun cast a narrow beam of light down to the valley floor lying at a dizzying depth below us. Where there had been nothing a moment ago but fathomless gloom, there now shone a little village with a few orchards, meadows and fields, surrounded by black shadows but sparkling green like the Islands of the Blest, and as we walked down the road from the pass beside the pony and trap everything grew lighter and lighter, the mountain sides emerged from the darkness shining brightly, the fine grasses bending in the wind shimmered with light, the silvery willows gleamed down on the banks of the stream; before long we had descended from the barren heights and found ourselves among trees and bushes again, beneath the softly rustling oaks and maples, and rowans already laden with red berries. Once, I think when I was nine, I went away with Elias to a place in South Wales where the flanks of the mountains had been ripped open on both sides of the road, and the woods mauled and cut down. I don't remember the name of the village we reached at nightfall. It was surrounded by pithead stocks of coal spilling down into the alleys here and there. We had been given a room in the house of one of the church elders, from which there was a view of a winding-tower with a gigantic wheel turning now this way and now that in the gathering dusk, and further down the valley tall flames and showers of sparks shot high into the sky from the smelting furnaces of an iron and steel works, at regular intervals of about three or four minutes. When I was in bed Elias sat on a stool by the window, looking out in silence for a long time. I think that it was the sight of the valley first illuminated by the firelight, then sinking back into darkness, which inspired him to preach on a text from Revelation next morning, delivering a

Vyrnwy reservoir. As far as I can remember it was on the way back from one of his journeys to preach away from home, at either Abertridwr or Pont Llogel, that Elias stopped the pony-trap on the banks of this lake and walked out with me to the middle of the dam, where he told me about his family home lying down there at a depth of about a hundred feet under the dark water, and not just his own family home but at least forty other houses and farms, together with the church of St John of Jerusalem, three chapels and three pubs, all of them drowned when the dam was finished in the autumn of 1888. In the years before its submersion, so Elias had told him, said Austerlitz, Llanwddyn had been particularly famous for its games of football on the village green when the full moon shone in summer, often lasting all night and played by over ten dozen youths and men of almost every age, some of them from neighbouring villages. The story of the football games of Llanwddyn occupied my imagination for a long time, said Austerlitz, first and foremost, I am sure, because Elias never told me anything else about his own life either before or afterwards. At this one moment on the Vyrnwy dam when, intentionally or unintentionally, he allowed me a glimpse into his clerical heart, I felt for him so much that he, the righteous man, seemed to me like the only survivor of the deluge which had destroyed Llanwddyn, while I imagined all the others – his parents, his brothers and sisters, his relations, their neighbours, all the other villagers – still down in the depths, sitting in their houses and walking along the road, but unable to speak and with their eyes opened far too wide. This notion of mine about the sub-aquatic existence of the people of Llanwddyn also had something to do with the album which Elias first showed me on our return home that evening, containing several photographs of his birthplace, now sunk beneath the water. As there were no

other pictures of any kind in the manse, I leafed again and again though these few photographs, which came into my own possession only much later along with the Calvinist calendar, until the people looking out of them, the blacksmith in his leather apron, Elias's father the sub-postmaster, the shepherd walking along the village street with his sheep, and most of all the girl sitting in a chair in the garden with her little dog on her lap, became as familiar to me as if I were living with

them down at the bottom of the lake. At night, before I fell asleep in my cold room, I often felt as if I too had been submerged in that dark water, and like the poor souls of Vyrnwy must keep my eyes wide open to catch a faint glimmer of light far above me, and see the reflection, broken by ripples, of the stone tower standing in such fearsome isolation on the wooded bank. Sometimes I even imagined that I had seen one or other of the people from the photographs in the album walking down the road in Bala, or out in the fields, particularly around noon on hot summer days, when there was no one else about and the air flickered hazily. Elias said I was not to speak of such things, so instead I spent every free moment I could with Evan the cobbler, whose workshop was not far from the manse and who had a reputation for seeing ghosts. I also learned Welsh from Evan, picking it up very quickly, because I liked his stories much better than the endless psalms and biblical verses I had to learn by heart for Sunday school. Unlike Elias, who always connected illness and death with tribulations, just punishment and guilt, Evan told tales of the dead who had been struck down by fate untimely, who knew they had been cheated of what was due to them and tried to return to life. If you had an eye for them they were to be seen quite often, said Evan. At first glance they seemed to be normal people, but when you looked more closely their faces would blur or flicker slightly at the edges. And they were usually a little shorter than they had been in life, for the experience of death, said Evan, diminishes us, just as a piece of linen shrinks when you first wash it. The dead almost always walked alone, but they did sometimes go around in small troops; they had been seen wearing brightly coloured uniforms or wrapped in grey cloaks, marching up the hill above the town to the soft beat of a drum, and only a little taller than the walls round the fields through which they went. Evan told me the story of how his grandfather once had to step aside on the road from Frongastell to Pyrsau to let one of these ghostly processions pass by when it caught up with him. It had consisted entirely of beings of dwarfish stature who strode on at a fast pace, leaning forward slightly and talking to each other in reedy voices. Hanging from a hook on the wall above Evan's low work-bench, said Austerlitz, was the black veil that his grandfather had taken from the bier when the small figures muffled in their cloaks carried it past him, and it was certainly Evan, said Austerlitz, who once told me that nothing but a piece of silk like that separates us from the next world. It is a fact that through all the years I spent at the manse in Bala I never shook off the feeling that something very obvious, very manifest in itself was hidden from me. Sometimes it was as if I were in a dream and trying to perceive reality; then again I felt as if an invisible twin brother were walking beside me, the reverse of a shadow, so to speak. And I suspected that some meaning relating to myself lay behind the Bible stories I was given to read in Sunday school from my sixth year onwards, a meaning quite different from the sense of the printed words as I ran my index finger along the lines. I can still see myself, said Austerlitz, muttering intently and spelling out the story of Moses again and again from the large-print children's edition of the Bible Miss Parry had given me when I had been set to learn by heart the chapter about the confounding of the languages of the earth, and succeeded in reciting it correctly and with good expression. I have only to turn a couple of pages of that book, said Austerlitz, to remember how anxious I felt at the time when I read the tale of the daughter of Levi, who made an ark of bulrushes and daubed it with slime and with pitch, placed the child in the ark and laid it among the reeds by the side of the water – *yn yr hesg ar fin yr afon*, I think that was how it ran. Further on in the story of Moses, said Austerlitz, I particularly liked the episode where the children of Israel cross a terrible wilderness, many days' journey long and wide, with nothing in sight but sky and sand as far as the eye can see. I tried to picture the pillar of cloud going before the people on their wanderings 'to lead them the way', as the Bible puts it, and I immersed myself, forgetting all around me, in a full-page illustration showing the desert of Sinai looking just like the part of Wales where I grew up, with bare mountains crowding close together and a grey-hatched background, which I took sometimes for the sea and sometimes for the air above it. And indeed, said Austerlitz on a later occasion when he showed me his Welsh children's Bible, I knew that my proper place was among the tiny figures populating the camp. I examined every square inch of the

illustration, which seemed to me uncannily familiar. I thought I could make out a stone quarry in a
rather lighter patch on the steep slope of the
mountain over to the right, and I seemed to see a
railway track in the regular curve of the lines
below it. But my mind dwelt chiefly on the fenced
square in the middle and the tent-like building at
the far end, with a cloud of white smoke above it.
Whatever may have been going on inside me at
the time, the children of Israel's camp in the
wilderness was closer to me than life in Bala,
which I found more incomprehensible every day,
or at least, said Austerlitz, that is how it strikes me
now. That evening in the bar of the Great Eastern
Hotel Austerlitz also told me that there was no
wireless set or newspaper in the manse in Bala. I
don't know that Elias and his wife Gwendolyn
ever mentioned the fighting on the continent of
Europe, he said. I couldn't imagine any world
outside Wales. Only after the end of the war did
this state of affairs begin to change. A new epoch
seemed to dawn with the victory celebrations,
when even in Bala there was dancing in the streets,
which were decked with brightly coloured bunt-
ing. For me, it began when I first broke the ban on

going to the cinema, and after that I used to watch the newsreel from the cubby-hole occupied by the film projectionist Owen, one of the three sons of the visionary Evan. Around the same time Gwendolyn's state of health deteriorated, almost imperceptibly at first but then with increasing speed. She, who had always kept everything in the most painfully neat order, began to neglect first the house and then herself. She simply stood in the kitchen, looking helpless, and when Elias prepared a meal as best he could she would eat almost nothing. Her illness was certainly the reason why I was sent to a private school near Oswestry in the autumn term of 1946, when I was twelve years old. Like most such educational establishments, Stower Grange was the most unsuitable place imaginable for an adolescent. The headmaster, a man called Penrith-Smith, who wandered aimlessly about the school buildings in his dusty gown all day from early morning until late at night, was hopelessly forgetful and absent-minded, and the rest of the teaching staff in that immediate post-war period were also a curious collection of oddities, most of them over sixty or suffering from some affliction. School life ran more or less of its own accord, not so much thanks to the masters who taught us at Stower Grange as in spite of them, and certainly not by virtue of any particular ethos but through customs and traditions, a number of them positively oriental in character, going back over many generations of pupils. There were all kinds of forms of major tyranny and minor despotism, forced labour, enslavement, serfdom, the bestowal and withdrawal of privileges, hero-worship, ostracism, the imposition of penalties and the granting of reprieves, and by dint of these the pupils, without any supervision, governed themselves and indeed the entire school, not excluding the masters. Even when Penrith-Smith, a remarkably kindly man, did have to chastise one of us in his office for some reason which had been brought to his notice, you could easily have gained the impression that the victim was temporarily granting the headmaster who inflicted the punishment a privilege due in fact only to him, the boy who had reported to take it. Sometimes, particularly at weekends, it seemed as if all the masters had gone away leaving the pupils in their care to their own devices in the school, which was at least two miles outside said Austerlitz, I myself found my years at Stower Grange a time not of imprisonment but of liberation. While most of us, even those who tormented their contemporaries, crossed off the days on the calendar until they could go home, I would have preferred never to return to Bala at all. From the very first week I realized that for all the adversities of the school it was my only escape route, and I immediately did all I could to find my way around its strange jumble of countless unwritten rules, and the often almost carnivalesque lawlessness that prevailed. It was a great advantage that I soon began to distinguish myself on the rugby field, perhaps because a dull pain always present within me, although I was unaware of it at the time, enabled me to lower my head and make my way through ranks of opponents better than any of my fellow pupils. The fearlessness I displayed in rugger matches, as I remember them always played under a cold winter sky or in pouring rain, very soon gave me special status without my having to try for it by other means, such as recruiting vassals or enslaving weaker boys. Another crucial factor in my good progress at school was the fact that I never found reading and studying a burden.

long as I could remember. Gwendolyn had gone further downhill during my two months' absence. She now lay in bed all day looking fixedly up at the ceiling. Elias came in to see her for a while every morning and every evening, but neither he nor Gwendolyn spoke a single word. It seems to me now, looking back, said Austerlitz, as if they were slowly being killed by the chill in their hearts. I don't know what kind of illness Gwendolyn died of, and I suspect that she herself could not have said. At least, she had no weapon against it but the curious compulsion which came over her several times a day, and perhaps during the night too, to powder herself with a kind of cheap talc from a large container standing on the little table beside her bed. Gwendolyn used such quantities of this powder, fine as dust and slightly greasy, that the linoleum floor around her bed, and soon the whole room and the corridors of the upper storey as well, were covered with a white layer, slightly sticky because of the damp air. I only recently remembered this white pall over the manse, said Austerlitz, when I was reading the reminiscences of his childhood and youth by a Russian writer who describes a similar mania for powder in his grandmother, a lady who, although she spent most of her time lying on a sofa nourishing herself almost exclusively on wine gums and almond milk, enjoyed an iron constitution and always slept with her window wide open, so that once, after a night of stormy weather, she woke up in the morning under a blanket of snow without coming to the slightest harm. However, it was different in the manse. The sick-room windows were kept closed, and the white powder which had settled on everything, grain by grain, and through which visible paths had now been trodden, was not at all like glittering snow. Rather, it resembled the ectoplasm that, as Evan had once told me, clairvoyants can produce from their mouths in great bubbles which then fall to the ground, where they soon dry and fall to dust. No, it was not newly fallen snow wafting around the manse; what filled it was something unpleasant, and I did not know where it came from, only much later and in another book finding for it the completely incomprehensible but to me, said Austerlitz, immediately enlightening term 'arsanical horror'. It was during the coldest winter in human memory that I came home for the second very far away, the sun shone faintly in the misty blue sky, the dying woman opened her eyes wide and would not move her glance from the weak light filtering through the window panes. Only when darkness fell did she lower her lids, and not long after that a gurgling sound began to emerge from her throat with every breath she took. I sat beside her all night, together with the minister. At dawn the stertorous breathing stopped. Gwendolyn's body arched slightly and then sank back again. It was a kind of tensing movement; I had felt it once before, when I picked up an injured rabbit from the headland of a field, and its heart stopped in my hand for fear. But directly after she had arched herself in death Gwendolyn's body seemed to shrink a little, reminding me of what Evan had told me. I saw her eyes sink back in their sockets, and her thin lips, now stretched tautly back, half-bared her crooked bottom teeth, while outside, for the first time in many days, the rose-coloured light of dawn touched the rooftops of Bala. I don't remember exactly how the rest of that day passed after she died, said Austerlitz. I think I was so exhausted that I lay down and slept very deeply for a very long time. When I got up again, Gwendolyn was already in her coffin, which stood on the four mahogany chairs in the front room. She was wearing her wedding dress, kept all these years in a trunk upstairs, and a pair of white gloves with a great many little mother of pearl buttons which I had never seen before. The sight of them brought tears into my eyes, the first tears I had ever shed in the manse. Elias was sitting beside the coffin keeping watch over the dead woman, while on his own out in the empty barn, which creaked with the frost, the young assistant minister who had ridden over from Corwen on a pony was rehearsing the sermon he would preach on the day of the funeral. Elias never recovered from his wife's death. Grief is not the right word for the condition into which he had fallen since she lay dying, said Austerlitz. Although I did not understand it at the time, as a boy of thirteen, I can see now that the unhappiness building up inside him had destroyed his faith just when he needed it most. When I came home again in the summer, it was weeks since he had been able to carry out his duties as a minister. He climbed into the pulpit once more, opened the Bible, and in a broken voice, as if reading to himself alone, suring diagnosis and made the whole wretched situation tolerable. — More than a year after my visit to the Denbigh asylum, at the beginning of the summer term of 1949, when we were just preparing for the exams which would determine our subsequent careers, said Austerlitz, resuming his narrative after a certain time, the headmaster Penrith-Smith summoned me to his study one morning. I can still see him in his frayed gown, wreathed in the blue tobacco smoke from his pipe, standing in the sunlight that slanted in through the small panes of the lead-glazed window and repeating several times in various ways, in his typically confused manner, that in the circumstances my conduct had been exemplary, truly exemplary, given the events of the last two years, and if in the next few weeks I came up to my teachers' expectations of me, which were undoubtedly justified, the Stower Grange trustees would award me a sixth-form scholarship. First, however, it was his duty to tell me that I must put not Dafydd Elias but Jacques Austerlitz on my exam papers. It appears, said Penrith-Smith, that this is your real name. My foster parents, with whom he had discussed the matter at length when

I entered the school, had meant to tell me about my origins in good time before the examinations, and if possible adopt me, but as matters now stood, said Penrith-Smith, that was unfortunately out of the question. All he knew himself was that the Eliases had taken me into their house at the beginning of the war, when I was only a little boy, so he could tell me no more. He was sure it would all be settled once Elias's condition improved. As far as the other boys are concerned, said Penrith-Smith, you remain Dafydd Elias for the time being. There's no need to let anyone know. It's just that you will have to put Jacques Austerlitz on your examination papers or else your work may be considered invalid. Penrith-Smith had written the name on a piece of paper, and when he handed it to me I could think of nothing to say, said Austerlitz, but 'Thank you, sir.' At first, what disconcerted me most was that I could connect no ideas at all with the word Austerlitz. If my new name had been Morgan or Jones, I could have related it to reality. I even knew the name Jacques from a French nursery rhyme. But I had never heard of an Austerlitz before, and from the first I was convinced that no one else bore that name, no one in Wales, or in the Isles, or anywhere else in the world. And since I began investigating my own history some years ago, I have never in fact come upon another Austerlitz, not in the telephone books of London or Paris, Amsterdam or Antwerp. But not long ago, turning on the wireless, I happened upon an announcer saying that Fred Astaire, of whom I had previously known nothing at all, was born with the surname of Austerlitz. Astaire's father, who according to this surprising radio programme came from Vienna, had worked as a master brewer in Omaha, Nebraska, where Astaire was born, and from the veranda of the Austerlitz family's house you could hear freight trains being shunted back and forth in the city's marshalling yard. Astaire is reported to have said later that this constant, uninterrupted shunting sound, and the ideas it suggested of going on a long railroad journey, were his only early childhood memories. And just a couple of days after I chanced in this way upon the story of a man entirely unknown to me, Austerlitz added, a neighbour who describes herself as a passionate reader told me that in Kafka's diaries she had found a small, bow-legged himself. The Emperor's childhood in Ajaccio, his studies at the military academy of Brienne, the siege of Toulon, the stresses and strains of the Egyptian expedition and his return over a sea full of enemy ships, the crossing of the Great St Bernard, the battles of Marengo, Jena and Auerstedt, of Eylau and Friedland, of Wagram, Leipzig and Waterloo – Hilary brought it all vividly to life for us, partly by recounting the course of these events, often passing from plain narrative to dramatic descriptions and then on to a kind of impromptu performance distributed among several different roles, from one to another of which he switched back and forth with astonishing virtuosity, and partly by studying the gambits of Napoleon and his opponents with the cold intelligence of a non-partisan strategist, surveying the entire landscape of those years from above with an eagle eye, as he once and not without pride remarked. Most of us were deeply impressed by Hilary's history lessons, not least, said Austerlitz, because very often, probably owing to his suffering from slipped discs, he gave them while lying on his back on the floor, nor did we find this at all comic, for it was at such times that Hilary spoke with particular clarity and authority. His undoubted *pièce de résistance* was the battle of Austerlitz. He spoke on it at length, describing the terrain, the highway leading east from Brünn to Olmütz, with the hilly Moravian countryside on its left and the Pratzen heights on its right, the curious cone-shaped mountain which reminded the veterans in the Napoleonic army of the Egyptian pyramids, the villages of Bellwitz, Skolnitz and Kobelnitz, the game park and pheasant enclosure, the watercourse of the Goldbach and the pools and lakes to the south, the French encampment as well as that of the ninety thousand Allies, which extended over a length of nine miles. Hilary told us, said Austerlitz, how at seven in the morning the peaks of the highest hills emerged from the mist like islands in a sea and, as the day gradually grew brighter over the rounded hill-tops, the milky haze in the valleys became noticeably denser. The Russian and Austrian troops had come down from the mountain sides like a slow avalanche, and soon, increasingly unsure where they were going, were wandering around on the slopes and in the meadows below, while the French, in a single onslaught, captured the now how, or simply saying what the battlefield was like at nightfall, with the screams and groans of the wounded and dying. In the end all anyone could ever do was sum up the unknown factors in the ridiculous phrase, 'The fortunes of battle swayed this way and that', or some similarly feeble and useless cliché. All of us, even when we think we have noted every tiny detail, resort to set pieces which have already been staged often enough by others. We try to reproduce the reality, but the harder we try, the more we find the pictures that make up the stock-in-trade of the spectacle of history forcing themselves upon us: the fallen drummer boy, the infantryman shown in the act of stabbing another, the horse's eye starting from its socket, the invulnerable Emperor surrounded by his generals, a moment frozen still amidst the turmoil of battle. Our concern with history, so Hilary's thesis ran, is a concern with pre-formed images already imprinted on our brains, images at which we keep staring while the truth lies elsewhere, away from it all, somewhere as yet undiscovered. I myself, added Austerlitz, in spite of all the accounts of it I have read, remember only the picture of the final defeat of the Allies that I told him the secret of my real name. It was some time before he was able to calm down. He struck his forehead again and again, breaking into exclamations of astonishment, as if Providence had finally sent him the pupil he had always wanted. For the rest of my time at Stower Grange, Hilary supported and encouraged me in every possible way. I owe it to him first and foremost, said Austerlitz, that I far outstripped the rest of my year in our final examinations in history, Latin, German and French, and could go on my own way into freedom, as I confidently thought at the time, provided with a generous scholarship. When we said goodbye André Hilary gave me a present from his collection of Napoleonic memorabilia, a gold-framed piece of dark card on which, behind shining glass, were fixed three rather fragile willow leaves from a tree on the island of St Helena, along with a scrap of lichen resembling a pale sprig of coral taken by one of Hilary's forebears, as the tiny caption said, from the heavy granite tombstone of Marshal Ney on 31 July 1830. This memento, worth nothing in itself, is still in my possession, said Austerlitz. It means more to me than almost any other picture, first because despite their fragility the relics preserved in it, the lichen and the dried lanceolate willow leaves, have remained intact for more than a century, but also because it reminds me daily of Hilary, without whom I would surely never have been able to emerge from the shadows of the manse in Bala. Moreover, it was Hilary who, after my foster-father's death in the Denbigh asylum early in 1954, undertook the task of winding up his meagre estate and then set on foot the process of my naturalization, which in view of the fact that Elias had obliterated every indication of my origin involved a good deal of difficulty. When I was studying at Oriel, like Hilary himself before me, he visited me regularly, and we took every opportunity of making excursions to the deserted and dilapidated country houses to be found all around Oxford, as elsewhere, in the post-war years. While I was still at school, said Austerlitz, as well as Hilary's support my friendship with Gerald Fitzpatrick in particular helped me to overcome the self-doubts that sometimes oppressed me. In line with the usual practice at public schools, Gerald was assigned to me as a fag when I entered the sixth form. It was his job to keep my room tidy, clean my boots, and bring the tray with the tea things. From the first day, when he asked me for one of the new photographs of the rugger team where I featured to the extreme right of the front row, I realized that Gerald felt as isolated as I did, said Austerlitz, who scarcely a week after our reunion at the Great Eastern Hotel sent me a postcard copy of the picture he had mentioned, without further comment. On that December

evening, however, in the hotel bar, which was quiet now, Austerlitz went on to tell me more about Gerald, and how he had suffered from awful homesickness ever since his arrival at Stower Grange, entirely against the grain of his naturally cheerful disposition. All the time, said

Austerlitz, in every free moment he had, he was rearranging the things he had brought from home in his tuck-box, and once, not long after he became my fag, I found him at the end of a corridor one dreary Saturday afternoon, with the autumn rain pouring down outside, trying to set fire to a pile of newspapers stacked on the stone floor beside the open door which led into a back yard. I saw his small, crouched figure in the grey light behind him, and the little flames licking around the edges of the newspaper, but the fire would not burn properly. When I asked what he thought he was doing, he said he wanted to make a huge blaze, and would not mind if the whole school were reduced to a pile of rubble and ashes. After that I kept an eye on Gerald. I let him off tidying my room and cleaning my boots, and I made the tea myself and shared it with him, a breach of regulations regarded with disapproval by most of my fellow pupils and my house-master himself, rather as if it were against the natural order of things. In the evenings Gerald often accompanied me to the dark-room where, at this time, I was making my first experiments with photography. This little cubby-hole behind the chemistry lab had not been used for years, but the wall cupboards and drawers still held several boxes with rolls of film, a large supply of photographic paper and a miscellaneous collection of cameras, including an Ensign such as I myself owned later. From the outset my main concern was with the shape and the self-contained nature of discrete things, the curve of banisters on a staircase, the moulding of a stone arch over a gateway, the tangled precision of the blades in a tussock of dried grass. I took hundreds of such photographs at Stower Grange, most of them in square format,

 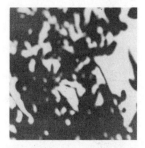

but it never seemed to me right to turn the viewfinder of my camera on people. In my photographic work I was always especially entranced, said Austerlitz, by the moment when the shadows of reality, so to speak, emerge out of nothing on the exposed paper, as memories do in the middle of the night, darkening again if you try to cling to them, just like a photographic print left in the developing bath too long. Gerald enjoyed helping me, and I can still see him, a head shorter than I was, standing beside me in the dark-room, which was dimly illuminated only by the little reddish light, holding the photographs in tweezers and swishing them back and forth in a sink full of water. He often told me about his family on these occasions, and most of all he liked talking about the three homing pigeons who would be expecting his return, he thought, as eagerly as he usually awaited theirs. Gerald's Uncle Alphonso had given him these pigeons a year ago for his tenth birthday, said Austerlitz, two of them a slaty blue, one snow-white. Whenever possible, if someone was going to Bala or Aberystwyth by car, he would send his three pigeons to be freed at a distance, and they always infallibly found their way

blue, and the sky where the clouds, coming in from the sea, always drove eastwards. Scraps of steam vapour flew past outside; you could hear the engine whistling and feel the air cool on your forehead. Never have I travelled better, said Austerlitz, than on this journey of seventy miles at the most, which took us three and a half hours. When we stopped at Bala, the half way station, of course I could not help thinking back to my time in the manse, visible up there on its hill, yet it always seemed to me inconceivable that I had really been among its unhappy inhabitants for almost the whole of my life. And every time I set eyes on Lake Bala, particularly when its surface was churned up by the wind in winter, I remembered the story Evan the cobbler had told me, about the two headstreams of Dwy Fawr and Dwy Fach which are said to flow right through the lake, far down in its dark depths, never mingling their waters with its own. The two rivers, according to Evan, said Austerlitz, were called after the only human beings not drowned but saved from the biblical deluge in the distant past. At the far end of Lake Bala the railway line passed over a low anticline into the Afon Mawddach valley. The mountains were higher now, coming down closer and closer to the tracks until you reached Dolgellau, where they retreated again, and gentler slopes fell to the estuary of the Mawddach, which reaches far inland like a fjord. Finally, when we left the southern bank and crawled to the opposite side over the bridge, almost a mile long and supported on mighty posts of oak, on our right the river bed, inundated by the sea at high tide and looking like a mountain lake, and on our left Barmouth Bay stretching to the bright horizon, I felt so joyful that I often scarcely knew where to look first. Adela used to fetch us from Barmouth station, usually in the little black-painted pony-trap, and then it was only half an hour before the gravel of the drive up to Andromeda Lodge was crunching under our wheels, the bay pony stopped, and we could get down and enter into our holiday refuge. The two-storey house, built of pale-grey brick, was protected to the north and north-east by the Llawr Llech hills, which fall steeply away at this point. To the south-west the terrain lay open in a wide semi-circle, so that from the forecourt of the house you had a view of the full length of the estuary from Dolgellau to

Barmouth, while these places themselves were excluded from the panorama, which was almost devoid of human habitations, by a rocky outcrop on one side and a laurel-grown hill on the other. Only on the far side of the river could the little village of Arthog be seen – in certain atmospheric conditions, said Austerlitz, you might have thought it an eternity away – infinitesimally small, with the shadowy side of Cader Idris rising behind it to a height of almost three thousand feet above the shimmering sea. While the climate of the entire area was remarkably mild, temperatures in this especially favoured place were a couple of degrees higher even than the Barmouth average. The garden, which had run completely wild during the war years and went up the slope at the back of the house, contained plants and shrubs that I had never seen in Wales before: giant rhubarb and New Zealand ferns taller than a grown man, water lettuce and camellias, thickets of bamboo and palms. And a brook tumbled down over a rocky wall to the valley, its white spray constantly pervading the dappled twilight under the leafy canopy of the tall trees. But it was not only the plants, natives of warmer climates, that and walking along the ground, always active and always, or that was the impression they gave, intent upon some purpose or other. In fact they were very like human beings in many ways. You might hear them sigh, laugh, sneeze and yawn. They cleared their throats before beginning to converse in their own cockatoo language, they showed themselves alert, scheming, mischievous and sly, deceitful, malicious, vindictive and quarrelsome. They liked certain people, particularly Adela and Gerald, and persecuted others with downright malice, for instance the Welsh housekeeper who seldom showed her face out of doors. They seemed to know exactly when she would be going to chapel, always wearing a black hat and carrying a black umbrella, and on these occasions they lay in wait to screech at her in the most obnoxious way. They also reflected human society in the way they ganged up together in ever-changing groups, or then again paired off in couples sitting side by side as if they knew nothing but harmony and were forever inseparable. They even had their own cemetery, with a long row of graves in a clearing surrounded by strawberry trees, and one of the rooms on the upper floor of

Andromeda Lodge had in it what was obviously a purpose-built wall cupboard, full of dark-green cardboard boxes containing a number of dead birds of species related to the cockatoos, their red-chested or yellow-headed brothers, Hyacinth and Scarlet Macaws, Ruby Lorikeets and Blue-winged Parrotlets, Horned Parakeets and Ground Parrots, all brought back by Gerald's great-grandfather or great-great-grandfather from his circumnavigation of the globe, or alternatively ordered from a trader called Théodore Grace in Le Havre for a few guineas or louis d'or, as noted on the provenances placed inside the boxes. The finest of all these birds, in a collection which also included some native woodpeckers, wrynecks, kites and orioles, was the African Grey Parrot. I can still see the inscription on his green cardboard sarcophagus: Jaco, *Ps. erithacus L.* He came from the Congo and had reached the great age of sixty-six in his Welsh exile, as his obituary recounted, adding that he had been very tame and trusting, was a quick learner, chattered away to himself and others, could whistle entire songs and had composed some too, but best of all he liked to mimic the voices of children and to have them teach him

new words. His one bad habit was that if no one
gave him any apricot kernels and hard nuts, which
he could crack open with the greatest ease, he
went about in a bad temper chewing and shredding the furniture. Gerald often took this special
parrot out of his box. He was about nine inches
long, and as his name suggests had ash-grey
plumage, as well as a carmine tail, a black beak,
and a pale face that you might have thought was
marked by deep grief. Indeed, Austerlitz went on,
there was some kind of cabinet of natural curiosi-
ties in almost every room at Andromeda Lodge:
cases with multiple drawers, some of them glass-
fronted, where the roundish eggs of parrots were
arranged in their hundreds; collections of shells,
minerals, beetles and butterflies; slowworms,

adders and lizards preserved in formaldehyde; snail shells and sea urchins, crabs and shrimps, and large herbaria containing leaves, flowers and grasses. Adela had once told him, said Austerlitz, that the transformation of Andromeda Lodge into a kind of natural-history museum had begun in 1869, when Gerald's parrot-collecting ancestor made the acquaintance of Charles Darwin, then working on his study of the Descent of Man in a rented house not far from Dolgellau. Darwin had paid frequent visits to the Fitzpatricks of Andromeda Lodge in those days, and according to a family tradition he always praised the wonderful view from the house. It was from the same period, according to Adela, said Austerlitz, that the schism in the Fitzpatrick clan dated, a schism continuing to the present day, whereby one of the two sons in every generation abandoned the Catholic faith and became a natural scientist. For instance Aldous, Gerald's father, had been a botanist, while his brother Evelyn, over twenty years his senior, clung to the traditional Papist creed regarded in Wales as the worst of all per-versions. In fact the Catholic line of the family had always been represented by its crazier and more

eccentric members, as the case of Uncle Evelyn clearly illustrated. At the time when I was spending many weeks every year with the Fitzpatricks as Gerald's guest, said Austerlitz, Evelyn was perhaps in his mid-fifties, but was so crippled by Bechterew's disease that he looked like an old man, and could walk only with the greatest difficulty, bending right over. For that very reason, however, and to prevent his joints from seizing up entirely, he was always on the move in his rooms on the top floor, where a kind of handrail had been fitted along the walls, like the barre in a ballet school. He held on to this handrail as he inched his way forward, moaning quietly, his head and bent torso scarcely higher than his hand on the rail. It took him a good hour to make the rounds of his quarters, from the bedroom into the living-room, out of the living-room into the corridor, and from the corridor back to the bedroom. Gerald, who had already developed an aversion to the Roman faith, once claimed, said Austerlitz, that Uncle Evelyn had grown so crooked out of sheer miserliness, which he justified to himself by reflecting that he sent the money he did not spend in any given week, usually amounting to twelve or thirteen shillings, as a donation to the Mission to the Congo for the salvation of black souls still languishing in unbelief. There were no curtains or other furnishings in Evelyn's rooms, since he did not want to make unnecessary use of anything, even if it had been acquired long ago and simply had to be brought from another part of the house. Years before, he had had a narrow strip of lino- leum laid on the wooden floor where he walked beside the walls, to spare the wood, and his drag- ging footsteps had worn the linoleum so thin that you could make out almost nothing of its original flower pattern. Not until the temperature on the thermometer beside the window had dropped to below fifty degrees Fahrenheit for several days running was the housekeeper allowed to light a tiny fire in the hearth, a fire burning almost no fuel at all. To save electricity, Evelyn always went to bed when darkness fell, which meant around four in the afternoon in winter, although lying down was perhaps even more painful for him than walking, so that as a rule, despite his exhausted state after his constant perambulations, it was a long time before he could get to sleep. Then, through the grille of a ventilation shaft that linked

before your eyes. The faint images that Alphonso transferred on to paper, said Austerlitz, were barely sketches of pictures — here a rocky slope, there a small bosky thicket or a cumulus cloud — fragments, almost without colour, fixed with a tint made of a few drops of water and a grain of malachite green or ash blue. I remember, said Austerlitz, how Alphonso once told his great-nephew and me that everything was fading before our eyes, and that many of the loveliest of colours had already disappeared, or existed only where no one saw them, in the submarine gardens fathoms deep below the surface of the sea. In his child-hood, he said, he used to walk beside the chalk cliffs of Devon and Cornwall, where hollows and basins have been carved and cut out of the rock by the breakers over millions of years, admiring the endless diversity of the semi-sentient marvels oscillating between the vegetable, animal and mineral kingdoms, the zooids and corallines, sea anemones, sea fans and sea feathers, the antho-zoans and crustaceans over which the tide washed twice a day while long fronds of seaweed swayed around them, and which then, as the water went out, revealed their wonderfully iridescent life in surrounded by heather and lit it than the moths, not one of which we had seen during our climb, came flying in as if from nowhere, describing thousands of different arcs and spirals and loops, until like snowflakes they formed a silent storm around the light, while others, wings whirring, crawled over the sheet spread under the lamp or else, exhausted by their wild circling, settled in the grey recesses of the egg boxes stacked in a crate by Alphonso to provide shelter for them. I do remember, said Austerlitz, that the two of us, Gerald and I, could not get over our amazement at the endless variety of these invertebrates, which are usually hidden from our sight, and that Alphonso let us simply gaze at their wonderful display for a long time, but I don't recollect now exactly what kinds of night-winged creatures landed there beside us, perhaps they were China-Marks, Dark Porcelains and Marbled Beauties, Scarce Silverlines or Burnished Brass, Green Foresters and Green Adelas, White Plumes, Light Arches, Old Ladies and Ghost Moths, but at any rate we counted dozens of them, so different in structure and appearance that neither Gerald nor I could grasp it all. Some had collars and cloaks, like elegant gentlemen on their way to the opera, said Gerald; some had a plain basic hue, but when they moved their wings showed a fantastic lining underneath, with oblique and wavy lines, shadows, crescent markings and lighter patches, freckles, zigzag bands, fringes and veining and colours you could never have imagined, moss green shot with blue, fox brown, saffron, lime yellow, satiny white, and a metallic gleam as of powdered brass or gold. Many of them were still resplendent in immaculate garments, others, their short lives almost over, had torn and ragged wings. Alphonso told us how each of these extravagant creatures had its own character, and that many of them lived only among alders, or on hot, stony slopes, in pastures on poor soil, or on moors. Describing their previous existence as larvae, he said that almost all caterpillars ate only one kind of food – the roots of couch grass, the leaves of sallow or barberry, withered bramble foliage – and they stuffed themselves with that chosen food, said Alphonso, until they became well-nigh senseless, whereas the moths ate nothing more at all for the rest of their lives, and were bent solely on the business of reproduction. They did sometimes seem to suffer thirst, and in periods of drought, when no dew had fallen at night for a long time, it was apparently known for them to set out together in a kind of cloud in search of the nearest river or stream, where they drowned in large numbers as they tried to settle on the flowing water. And I also remember what Alphonso said about the extraordinarily keen hearing of moths, said Austerlitz. They can make out the squeaking of bats from a great distance, and he, Alphonso, had himself noticed that in the evening, when the housekeeper came out into the yard to call her cat Enid in that shrill voice of hers, they always rose from the bushes and flew away into the darker trees. During the day, said Alphonso, they slept safely hidden under stones, or in cracks in the rock, in leaf litter on the ground or among foliage. Most of them are in a death-like state when you find them, and have to coax and quiver themselves back to life, crawling over the ground and jerkily moving their wings and legs before they are ready for flight. Their body temperature will then be thirty-six degrees, like that of mammals, and of dolphins and tunny fish swimming at full speed. Thirty-six degrees, according to Alphonso, has always proved the best natural level, a kind of magical threshold, and it had sometimes occurred to him, Alphonso, said Austerlitz, that all mankind's misfortunes were connected with its departure at some point in time from that norm, and with the slightly feverish, overheated condition in which we constantly found ourselves. On that summer night, said Austerlitz, we sat high above the estuary of the Mawddach in our hollow in the hills until daybreak, watching the moths fly to us, perhaps some ten thousand of them by Alphonso's estimate. The trails of light which they seemed to leave behind them in all kinds of curlicues and streamers and spirals, and which Gerald in particular admired, did not really exist, explained Alphonso, but were merely phantom traces created by the sluggish reaction of the human eye, appearing to see a certain afterglow in the place from which the insect itself, shining for only the fraction of a second in the lamplight, had already gone. It was such unreal phenomena, said Alphonso, the sudden incursion of unreality into the real world, certain effects of light in the landscape spread out before us, or in the eye of a beloved person, that

held fast by the tiny claws that stiffened in their last agony, until a draught of air detaches them and blows them into a dusty corner. Sometimes, seeing one of these moths that have met their end in my house, I wonder what kind of fear and pain they feel while they are lost. As Alphonso had told him, said Austerlitz, there is really no reason to suppose that lesser beings are devoid of sentient life. We are not alone in dreaming at night for, quite apart from dogs and other domestic creatures whose emotions have been bound up with ours for many thousands of years, the smaller mammals such as mice and moles also live in a world that exists only in their minds whilst they are asleep, as we can detect from their eye movements, and who knows, said Austerlitz, perhaps moths dream as well, perhaps a lettuce in the garden dreams as it looks up at the moon by night. I myself often felt as if I were dreaming during those weeks and months I spent at the Fitzpatricks' house, said Austerlitz, even in daylight. The view from the room with the blue ceiling which Adela always called mine did indeed verge on the unreal. I looked down from above on the treetops, mainly of cedars and parasol pines and resembling a green, hilly landscape going down from the road below the house to the river bank, I saw the dark folds of the mountain range on the other side of the river, and I spent hours looking out at the Irish Sea that was always changing with the time of day and the weather. How often I stood by the open window, unable to think coherently in the face of this spectacle, which was never the same twice. In the morning you saw the shadowy half of the world outside, the grey of the air lying in layers above the water. In the afternoon cumulus clouds often rose on the southwest horizon, their snow-white slopes and steep precipices displacing one another, towering above each other, reaching higher and higher, as high, Gerald once commented, said Austerlitz, as the one of the seats protected on three sides, like little cabins, from wind and weather, with your back to the land and looking out to sea. It was the end of a fine day in late summer, the fresh salty air blew around us, and in the evening light the tide came in, gleaming like a dense shoal of mackerel, flowing under the bridge and up the river, so swift and strong that you might have thought you were going the other way, out to the open sea in a boat. We all four sat there together in silence until the sun had set. Even the usually restless Toby, who had the same odd ruff of hair around his face as the little dog belonging to the girl in the Vyrnwy photograph, did not move at our feet, but looked up, rapt, at the heights where the light still lingered and large numbers of swallows were swooping through the air. After a while, when the dark dots had become tinier and tinier in their arching flight, Gerald asked whether we knew that these voyagers never slept on the earth. Once they had left their nests, he said, picking up Toby and tickling him under the chin, they never touched the ground again. As night fell they would rise two or three miles in the air and glide there, banking now to one side, now to the other, made an appointment to meet Austerlitz the next day Pereira, having inquired after my wishes, led me upstairs to the first floor and showed me into a room containing a great deal of wine-red velvet, brocade, and dark mahogany furniture, where I sat until almost three in the morning at a secretaire faintly illuminated by the street lighting – the cast-iron radiator clicked quietly, and only occasionally did a black cab drive past outside in Liverpool Street – writing down, in the form of notes and disconnected sentences, as much as possible of what Austerlitz had told me that evening. Next morning I woke late, and after breakfast I sat for some time reading the newspapers, where I found not only the usual home and international news, but also the story of an ordinary man who was overcome by such deep grief after the death of his wife, for whom he had cared devotedly during her long and severe illness, that he decided to end his own life by means of a guillotine which he had built himself in the square concrete area containing the basement steps at the back of his house in Halifax. As a craftsman, and having taken careful stock of other possible methods, he thought the guillotine the most reliable way of carrying out his plan, and sure enough, as the short report said, he had finally been found lying with his head cut off by such an instrument of decapitation. It was of uncommonly sturdy construction, with every tiny detail neatly finished, and a slanting blade which, as the reporter remarked, two strong men could scarcely have lifted. The pincers with which he had cut through the wire operating it were still in his rigid hand. Austerlitz had come to fetch me around eleven, and when I told him this story as we walked down to the river through Whitechapel and Shoreditch he said nothing for quite a long time, perhaps, I told myself reproachfully afterwards, because he felt it was tasteless of me to dwell on the absurd aspects of the case. Only on the river bank, where we stood for a while looking down at the grey-brown water rolling inland, did he say, looking straight at me as he sometimes did with wide and frightened eyes, that he could understand the Halifax carpenter very well, for what could be worse than to bungle even the end of an unhappy life? Then we walked the rest of the way in silence, going on downstream from Wapping and Shadwell to the quiet basins which reflect the towering office blocks of the Docklands area, and so to the foot tunnel running under the bend in the river. Over on the other side we climbed up through Greenwich Park to the Royal Observatory, which had scarcely any visitors apart from us on this cold day not long before Christmas. At least, I do not remember meeting anyone during the hours we spent there, both of us separately studying the ingenious observational instruments and measuring devices, quadrants and sextants, chronometers and regulators, displayed in the glass cases.

Only in the octagonal observation room above the quarters of the former Astronomers Royal, where Austerlitz and I gradually resumed the conversation we had broken off, did a solitary Japanese tourist appear in the doorway. He hovered there for a

while before he went all round the octagon once
and then quietly vanished again, following the
green arrow pointing the way. In this room, which
as Austerlitz commented was ideal for its purpose, I was surprised by the simple beauty of the
wooden flooring, made of planks of different
widths, and by the unusually tall windows, each
divided into a hundred and twenty-two lead-
framed square glass panes, through which long
telescopes were once turned on eclipses of the sun
and the moon, on the intersection of the orbits
of the stars with the line of the meridian, on the
Leonid meteorite showers and the long-tailed
comets flying through space. In accordance with his
usual custom, Austerlitz took a few photographs,
some of them of the snow-white stucco roses in the
frieze of flowers running round the ceiling, others
of the panorama of the city to the north and north-
west on the far side of the park, shot through the
leaded window panes, and while he was still busy
with his camera he embarked on a disquisition of
some length on time, much of which has remained
clear in my memory. Time, said Austerlitz in the
observation room in Greenwich, was by far the
most artificial of all our inventions, and in being

bound to the planet turning on its own axis was no less arbitrary than would be, say, a calculation based on the growth of trees or the duration required for a piece of limestone to disintegrate, quite apart from the fact that the solar day which we take as our guideline does not provide any precise measurement, so that in order to reckon time we have to devise an imaginary, average sun which has an invariable speed of movement and does not incline towards the equator in its orbit. If Newton thought, said Austerlitz, pointing through the window and down to the curve of the water around the Isle of Dogs glistening in the last of the daylight, if Newton really thought that time was a river like the Thames, then where is its source and into what sea does it finally flow? Every river, as we know, must have banks on both sides, so where, seen in those terms, where are the banks of time? What would be this river's qualities, qualities perhaps corresponding to those of water, which is fluid, rather heavy, and translucent? In what way do objects immersed in time differ from those left untouched by it? Why do we show the hours of light and darkness in the same circle? Why does time stand eternally still and motionless in one

thoroughly mendacious object, perhaps because I
have always resisted the power of time out of some
internal compulsion which I myself have never
understood, keeping myself apart from so-called
current events in the hope, as I now think, said
Austerlitz, that time will not pass away, has not
passed away, that I can turn back and go behind it,
and there I shall find everything as it once was, or
more precisely I shall find that all moments of time
have co-existed simultaneously, in which case none
of what history tells us would be true, past events
have not yet occurred but are waiting to do so at the
moment when we think of them, although that, of
course, opens up the bleak prospect of ever-lasting
misery and never-ending anguish. — It was around
three-thirty in the afternoon and dusk was gathering as I left the Observatory with Austerlitz. We
lingered for a while in the walled forecourt. Far
away, we could hear the hollow grinding of the
city, and the air was full of the drone of the great
planes flying low and as it seemed to me incredibly
slowly over Greenwich from the north-east, at
intervals of scarcely more than a minute, and then
disappearing again westwards towards Heathrow.
Like strange monsters going home to their dens to

plaster-coloured, a kind of excrescence or crust on the surface of the earth, and above the city the sky occupying half or more of the entire picture, perhaps with rain hanging down from the clouds in the far distance. I believe I first saw an example of these panoramas of Greenwich in one of the dilapidated country houses which, as I mentioned yesterday, I often visited with Hilary when I was studying at Oxford. I clearly remember, said Austerlitz, how on such an excursion, after walking for a long time in a park densely overgrown with young sycamore and birch trees, we came to a silent house of this kind, one of which on average, according to a calculation I made then, was being demolished every two or three days in the 1950s. We saw quite a number of houses at that time from which almost everything had been ripped out – the bookshelves, the panelling and banisters, the brass central-heating pipes and the marble fireplaces; houses with their roofs falling in, houses knee-deep in rubble, refuse and detritus, houses full of sheep and bird droppings and great lumps of plaster come down from the ceilings. Iver Grove, however, said Austerlitz, a house which stood in the middle of its wilderness of a park at the foot of a gentle south-facing slope, seemed largely intact, at least from the outside. None the less, as we paused on the broad stone steps which had been colonized by hart's-tongue ferns and other weeds and looked up at the blind windows, it seemed to us as if silent horror had seized upon the house at the prospect of its imminent and shameful end. Inside we found heaps of grain in one of the large ground-floor reception rooms, as if the place were a barn. In a second great hall, ornamented with baroque stucco work, hundreds of sacks of potatoes leaned against each other. We stood gazing at this sight for some time,

until – just as I was about to take some photographs – the owner of Iver Grove, who turned out to be a certain James Mallord Ashman, came towards the house along the western terrace. Fully understanding our interest in the buildings now everywhere falling into decay, he told us during a long conversation that after the family seat had been requisitioned for use as a convalescent home during the war years, the expense of putting it back into any kind of order, however makeshift, had been far beyond his means, so that he had been obliged to move to Grove Farm, which belonged to the estate and lay at the other end of the park, and to work the land himself. Hence, so Ashman told us, said Austerlitz, the sacks of potatoes and the grain on the floor. Iver Grove had been built around 1780 by one of Ashman's ancestors, said Austerlitz, a man who suffered from insomnia and withdrew into the observatory he had built at the top of the house to devote himself to various astronomical studies, particularly selenography or the delineation of the moon, and consequently, as Ashman told us, he had also been in frequent contact with John Russell of Guildford, a miniaturist and artist in pastels famous beyond the frontiers of England, who for several decades at this period was working on a map of the moon laid out over an area measuring five feet by five feet, and easily surpassing all earlier depictions of the earth's satellite in its precision and beauty, those of Riccioli and Cassini and those of Tobias Mayer and Hevelius alike. On nights when the moon did not rise or was veiled by cloud, said Ashman, when he had finished showing us round his house and we entered the billiards room, on such nights his ancestor used to play frame after frame of billiards against himself in this retreat, which he had equipped specially for the purpose, often until the dawn of day. Since his death on New Year's Eve 1813, no one had ever picked up a cue in the games room, said Ashman, not his grandfather or his father or himself, Ashman, let alone one of the women, of course. And indeed, said Austerlitz, everything was exactly as it must have been a hundred and fifty years before. The mighty mahogany table, weighted down by the slate slabs embedded in it, stood in its place unmoved; the scoring apparatus, the gold-framed looking-glass on the wall, the stands for the cues and their extension shafts, the cabinet full of drawers containing the ivory balls, the chalks, brushes, polishing cloths and everything else the billiard player requires, had never been touched again or changed in any way. Over the mantelpiece hung an engraving after Turner's *View from Greenwich Park*, and the records book in which the

selenographer, under the rubric Ashman vs. Ashman, had entered all games won or lost against himself in his fine curving hand still lay open on a tall desk. The inside shutters had always been kept closed, and the light of day never entered the room. Evidently, said Austerlitz, this place had always remained so secluded from the rest of the house that for a century and a half scarcely so much as a gossamer-thin layer of dust had been able to settle on the cornices, the black and white square stone flags of the floor, and the green baize cloth stretched over the table, which seemed like a self-contained universe. It was as if time, which usually runs so irrevocably away, had stood still here, as if the years behind us were still to come, and I remember, said Austerlitz, that when we were standing in the billiards room of Iver Grove with Ashman, Hilary remarked on the curious confusion of emotions affecting even a historian in a room like this, sealed away so long from the flow of the hours and days and the succession of the generations. Ashman replied that in 1941, when the house was requisitioned, he himself had hidden the doors to the billiards room and the nurseries on the top floor of the house by putting in false walls and pushing large wardrobes in front of them, and when these partitions were taken down in the autumn of 1951 or 1952, and he entered the nursery again for the first time in ten years, it wouldn't have taken much, said Ashman, to overset his reason altogether. The mere sight of the model train with the green Great Western Railway carriages, and the Noah's Ark with the pairs of well-behaved animals saved from the Flood looking out of it, had made him feel as if the chasm of time were opening up before him, and as he ran his finger over the long row of notches he had carved in silent fury at the age of eight on the edge of his little bedside table, the day before he was sent off to preparatory school, Ashman remembered, the same rage had flared up in him again, and before he knew what he was about he found himself standing in the yard behind the house, firing his rifle several times at the little clock-tower on the coach-house, where the marks he made are visible on the clock-face to this day. Ashman and Hilary, Iver Grove and Andromeda Lodge, whatever my thoughts turn to, said Austerlitz as we descended the darkening grassy slopes of the park to the city lights which had now come on in a wide semi-circle before us, it all arouses in me a sense of disjunction, of having no ground beneath my feet. I think it was in early October 1957, he continued abruptly after some time, when I was on the point of going to Paris to pursue the studies of architectural history on which I had embarked the previous year at the Courtauld Institute, that I last visited the Fitzpatricks in Barmouth for the double funeral of Uncle Evelyn and Great-Uncle Alphonso. They had died almost within a day of each other, Alphonso of a stroke as he was picking up his favourite apples out in the garden, Evelyn in his icy bed, cramped with pain and anguish. Autumn mists filled the whole valley on the morning of the burial of these two very different men, Evelyn always at odds with himself and the world, Alphonso animated by a cheerfully equable temperament. Just as the funeral procession began moving towards Cutiau cemetery, the sun broke through the hazy veils above the Mawddach, and a breeze blew along its banks. The few dark figures, the group of poplars, the flood of light over the water, the massif of Cader Idris on the far side of the river, these were the elements in a farewell scene which, curiously enough, I rediscovered a few weeks ago in one of the rapid watercolour sketches Turner often made, noting down what he saw either from life or looking back at the past later. This almost insubstantial picture, bearing the title of *Funeral at Lausanne*, dates from 1841, and thus from a time when Turner could hardly travel any more and dwelt increasingly on ideas of his own mortality, and perhaps for that very reason, when something like this little cortège in Lausanne emerged from his memory, he swiftly set down a

few brush-strokes in an attempt to capture visions which would melt away again the next moment. What particularly attracted me to Turner's water-colour, said Austerlitz, was not merely the similarity of the scene in Lausanne to the funeral at Cutiau, but the memory it prompted in me of my last walk with Gerald in the early summer of 1966, through the vineyards above Morges on the banks of Lake Geneva. During my subsequent studies of Turner's life and his sketchbooks I discovered the fact, entirely insignificant in itself but none the less one I found curiously moving, that in 1798 he, Turner, had himself visited the estuary of the Mawddach on a journey through Wales, and that at the time he was exactly the same age as I was at the funeral in Cutiau. As I speak of it now, said Austerlitz, it is as if I had been sitting in the south-facing drawing-room of Andromeda Lodge among the mourners only yesterday, as if I could still hear their quiet murmuring, and Adela saying she didn't know what she would do with herself now, all alone in that big house. Gerald, who was then in his last year of school and had come over from Oswestry especially for the funeral, told me about the lack of any improvement in conditions at Stower Grange, which he described as a horrible inkblot disfiguring the souls of its pupils for ever. He was kept from going mad, said Gerald, only by the fact that since joining the Air Cadet Corps he had been able to fly over the whole wretched place in a Chipmunk and get right away from it once a week. The further you can rise above the earth the

The trajectory it followed, always turning on its way although you could not have said how, was a streak of white drawn through the evening hour, and I could have sworn that Adela often hovered in the air just above the parquet floor for much longer than the force of gravity allowed. After our game we usually stayed in the ballroom for a little while, looking at the images cast on the wall opposite the tall, arched window by the last rays of the sun shining low through the moving branches of a hawthorn, until at last they were extinguished. There was something fleeting, evanescent about those sparse patterns appearing in constant succession on the pale surface, something which never went beyond the moment of its generation, so to speak, yet here, in this intertwining of sunlight and shadow always forming and re-forming, you could see mountainous landscapes with glaciers and ice-fields, high plateaux, steppes, deserts, fields full of flowers, islands in the sea, coral reefs, archipelagos and atolls, forests bending to the storm, quaking grass and drifting smoke. And once, I remember, said Austerlitz, as we gazed together at this slowly fading world, Adela leaned towards me and asked: Do you see the fronds of the palm trees, do you see my appointment in London and went to Cambridge to see Gerald, who had now finished his studies and was beginning his research work, Andromeda Lodge had been sold and Adela had gone to North Carolina with an entomologist called Willoughby. Gerald, who at the time had rented a cottage in the tiny village of Quy not far from Cambridge airfield and had bought a Cessna with his share of the proceeds from the sale of the property, kept coming back to his passion for flying in all our conversations, whatever their ostensible subjects. I remember, for instance, said Austerlitz, that once, when we were discussing our schooldays at Stower Grange, he told me at length how after I had gone up to Oxford he spent many of the endless hours of study at the school working out an ornithological system based, as its principal criterion, on the degree of a bird's aptitude for flight, and according to Gerald, said Austerlitz, whatever way he modified this system pigeons always led the field, not just for their speed in travelling very long distances but for their navigational abilities, which set them apart from all other living creatures. You can dispatch a pigeon from shipboard in the middle of a snow-storm over the North Sea, and if its strength holds out it will infallibly find its way home. To this day no one knows how these birds, sent off on their journey into so menacing a void, their hearts surely almost breaking with fear in their presentiment of the vast distances they must cover, make straight for their place of origin. At least, Gerald had said, the scientific explanations known to him claiming that pigeons take their bearings from the constellations, or air currents, or magnetic fields are not much more conclusive than the various theories he worked out himself as a boy of twelve, hoping that once he had solved this problem he would be able to make the pigeons fly the other way, for instance from their home in Barmouth to his place of exile in Oswestry, and he kept imagining them suddenly sailing down to him out of the sky, with sunlight filtered through the feathers of their motionless, outstretched wings, and landing with a faint coo in their throats on the sill of the window where, as he said, he often stood for hours on end. The sense of liberation he had felt when he first became aware of the lifting capacity of the air beneath him in one of the Cadet Corps planes, Gerald said, was indescribable, and he himself still remembered, added Austerlitz, how proud, indeed positively seen it before, apparently at a standstill but in truth turning slowly, with the constellations of the Swan, Cassiopeia, the Pleiades, the Charioteer, the Corona Borealis and all the rest almost lost in the shimmering dust of the myriads of nameless stars sprinkled over the sky. It was in the autumn of 1965, continued Austerlitz, who had drifted for some time in his memories, that Gerald began developing what we now know was his trail-blazing hypothesis on the so-called Eagle Nebula in the constellation of the Serpent. He spoke of huge regions of interstellar gas which, not unlike storm clouds, became concentrated into vast, billowing forms projecting several light years into the void, where new stars were born in a process of conden-sation steadily intensifying under the influence of gravity. I remember Gerald's saying that there

were positive nurseries of stars out there, a claim which I recently found confirmed in a newspaper report accompanying one of the spectacular photographs sent back to earth from the Hubble telescope on its further journey into space. At any rate, said Austerlitz, Gerald then moved from Cambridge to continue his work at an astrophysics research institute in Geneva, where I visited him several times, and as we walked out of the city together and along the banks of the lake I observed the way his ideas, like the stars themselves, gradually emerged from the whirling nebulae of his astrophysical fantasies. On one of these occasions Gerald also told me about the flights he had made over the gleaming, snow-covered mountains in his Cessna, over the volcanic peaks of the Puy-de-Dôme region, down the beautiful Garonne and on

to Bordeaux. I suppose it was inevitable that he would fail to come home from one of these flights, said Austerlitz. It was a bad day when I heard that he had crashed in the Savoy Alps, and perhaps that was the beginning of my own decline, a withdrawal into myself which became increasingly morbid and intractable with the passage of time.

*

Almost quarter of a year had passed before I next went to London and visited Austerlitz in his house in Alderney Street. On our parting in December we had agreed that I would wait to receive news from him. As the weeks went by I had felt less and less sure whether I would ever hear from him again, fearing at various times that I might have made a thoughtless remark, or offended him in some other way. It also occurred to me that, following his old custom, he might simply have gone away with some unknown purpose in mind and for an indefinite period. Had I realized at the time that for Austerlitz certain moments had no beginning or end, while on the other hand his whole life had sometimes seemed to him a blank point without duration, I would probably have waited more patiently. But at any rate, one day my mail included a picture postcard from the 1920s or 1930s showing a camp of white tents in the Egyptian desert, a picture taken during a campaign now remembered by no one, the message on the back saying merely

Saturday 19 March, Alderney Street, followed by a question mark and a capital *A* for Austerlitz. Alderney Street is quite a long way out in the East End of London. It is a remarkably quiet street running parallel to the main road not far from the Mile End junction, where there are always traffic jams and, on such Saturdays, market traders set up their stalls of clothes and fabrics on the pavements. Thinking back now, I see again a low block of flats like a fortress standing on the corner of the street; a garish green kiosk with its wares openly laid out,

photographs or others from his collection the wrong way up, as if playing a game of patience, and that then, one by one, he turned them over, always with a new sense of surprise at what he saw, pushing the pictures back and forth and over each other, arranging them in an order depending on their family resemblances, or withdrawing them from the game until either there was nothing left but the grey table top, or he felt exhausted by the constant effort of thinking and remembering and had to rest on the ottoman. I often lie here until late in the evening, feeling time roll back, said Austerlitz, as we passed into the sitting-room at the rear, where he lit the little gas fire and invited me to sit down on one of the chairs standing on either side of the hearth. This room too contained hardly any furniture; there were just the grey floorboards and the walls on which the light of the flickering blue flames was now cast in the gathering dusk. I can still hear the faint hiss of the gas, and I remember that while Austerlitz was making tea in the kitchen I sat entranced by the reflection of the little fire, which looked as if it were burning at some distance from the house on the other side of the glazed veranda doors, among the now almost pitch-black bushes in

- 168 -

the garden. When Austerlitz had brought the tea tray in and was holding slices of white bread on a toasting-fork in front of the blue gas flames, I said something about the incomprehensibility of mirror images, to which he replied that he often sat in this room after nightfall, staring at the apparently motionless spot of light reflected out there in the darkness, and when he did so he inevitably thought of a Rembrandt exhibition he had seen once, many years ago, in the Rijksmuseum in Amsterdam, where he had not felt inclined to linger before any of the large-scale masterpieces which have been reproduced over and over again, but instead stood for a long time looking at a small painting measuring at most nine by twelve inches, from the Dublin collection, as far as he remembered, which according to its label showed the Flight into Egypt, although he could make out neither Mary and Joseph, nor the child Jesus, nor the ass, but only a tiny flicker of fire in the middle of the gleaming black varnish of the darkness which, said Austerlitz, he could see in his mind's eye to this day. — But where, he continued, shall I take up my story? When I came back from France I bought this house for what today is the positively ridiculous sum of nine hundred and fifty pounds, and then I taught for almost thirty years until I took early retirement in 1991, partly, said Austerlitz, because of the inexorable spread of ignorance even to the universities, and partly because I hoped to set out on paper my investigations into the history of architecture and civilization, as had long been my intention. I might perhaps, Austerlitz said to me, have had some idea since our first conversations in Antwerp of the extent of his interests, the drift of his ideas and the nature of his observations and comments, always made extempore or first recorded in provisional form, but eventually covering thousands of pages. Even in Paris, said Austerlitz, I had thought of collecting my fragmentary studies in a book, although I constantly postponed writing it. The various ideas I entertained at different times of this book I was to write ranged from the concept of a systematically descriptive work in several volumes to a series of essays on such subjects as hygiene and sanitation, the architecture of the penal system, secular temples, hydrotherapy, zoological gardens, departure and arrival, light and shade, steam and gas, and so forth. However, even a first glance at the papers I had brought here from the Institute to

— 170 —

Alderney Street showed that they consisted largely of sketches which now seemed misguided, distorted, and of little use. I began to assemble and recast anything that still passed muster in order to re-create before my own eyes, as if in the pages of an album, the picture of the landscape, now almost immersed in oblivion, through which my journey had taken me. But the more I laboured on this

project over several months, the more pitiful did the results seem. I was increasingly overcome by a sense of aversion and distaste, said Austerlitz, at the mere thought of opening the bundles of papers and looking through the endless reams I had written in the course of the years. Yet reading and writing, he added, had always been his favourite occupation.

How happily, said Austerlitz, have I sat over a book in the deepening twilight until I could no longer make out the words and my mind began to wander, and how secure have I felt seated at the desk in my house in the dark night, just watching the tip of my pencil in the lamplight following its shadow, as if of its own accord and with perfect fidelity, while that shadow moved regularly from left to right, line by line, over the ruled paper. But now I found writing such hard going that it often took me a whole day to compose a single sentence, and no sooner had I thought such a sentence out, with the greatest effort, and written it down, than I saw the awkward falsity of my constructions and the inadequacy of all the words I had employed. If at times some kind of self-deception none the less made me feel that I had done a good day's work, then as soon as I glanced at the page next morning I was sure to find the most appalling mistakes, inconsistencies and lapses staring at me from the paper. However much or little I had written, on a subsequent reading it always seemed so fundamentally flawed that I had to destroy it immediately and begin again. Soon I could not even venture on the first step. Like a tightrope walker who has forgotten how to put one foot in front of the other, all I felt was the swaying of the precarious structure on which I stood, stricken with terror at the realization that the ends of the balancing pole gleaming far out on the edges of my field of vision were no longer my guiding lights, as before, but malignant enticements to me to cast myself into the depths. Now and then a train of thought did succeed in emerging with wonderful clarity inside my head, but I knew even as it formed that I was in no position to record it, for as soon as I so much as picked up my pencil the endless possibilities of language, to which I could once safely abandon myself, became a conglomeration of the most inane phrases. There was not an expression in the sentence but it proved to be a miserable crutch, not a word but it sounded false and hollow. And in this dreadful state of mind I sat for hours, for days on end with my face to the wall, tormenting myself and gradually discovering the horror of finding that even the smallest task or duty, for instance arranging assorted objects in a drawer, can be beyond one's power. It was as if an illness that had been latent in me for a long time were now threatening to erupt, as if some soul-destroying and inexorable force had fastened upon me and would gradually reaching further and further into the surrounding country, then I was like a man who has been abroad a long time and cannot find his way through this urban sprawl any more, no longer knows what a bus stop is for, or what a back yard is, or a street junction, an avenue or a bridge. The entire structure of language, the syntactical arrangement of parts of speech, punctuation, conjunctions, and finally even the nouns denoting ordinary objects were all enveloped in impenetrable fog. I could not even understand what I myself had written in the past – perhaps I could understand that least of all. All I could think was that such a sentence only appears to mean something, but in truth is at best a makeshift expedient, a kind of unhealthy growth issuing from our ignorance, something which we use, in the same way as many sea plants and animals use their tentacles, to grope blindly through the darkness enveloping us. The very thing which may usually convey a sense of purposeful intelligence – the exposition of an idea by means of a certain stylistic facility – now seemed to me nothing but an entirely arbitrary or deluded enterprise. I could see no connections any more, the sentences resolved themselves into a series of separate words,

the words into random sets of letters, the letters
into disjointed signs, and those signs into a bluegrey trail gleaming silver here and there, excreted
and left behind it by some crawling creature, and
the sight of it increasingly filled me with feelings
of horror and shame. One evening, said Austerlitz,
I gathered up all my papers, bundled or loose,
my notepads and exercise books, my files and
lecture notes, anything with my writing on it, and
carried the entire collection out of the house to
the far end of the garden, where I threw it on the
compost heap and buried it under layers of rotted
leaves and spadefuls of earth. For several weeks
afterwards, while I turned out the rooms of my
house and repainted the floors and walls, I did think
I felt some relief from the burden weighing down
on my life, but I soon realized that the shadows
were falling over me. Especially in the evening
twilight, which had always been my favourite time
of day, I was overcome by a sense of anxiety, dif-
fuse at first and then growing ever denser, through
which the lovely spectacle of fading colours turned
to a malevolent and lightless pallor, my heart felt
constricted in my chest to a quarter of its natural
size, until at last there remained only one idea in

my head: I must go to the third-floor landing of a certain building in Great Portland Street, where I had once had a strange turn after visiting a doctor's surgery, and throw myself over the banisters into the dark depths of the stairwell. It was impossible for me then to go and see any of my friends, who were not numerous in any case, or mix with other people in any normal way. The mere idea of listening to anyone brought on a wave of revulsion, while the thought of talking myself, said Austerlitz, was perhaps worse still, and as this state of affairs continued I came to realize how isolated I was and always have been, among the Welsh as much as among the English and French. It never occurred to me to wonder about my true origins, said Austerlitz, nor did I ever feel that I belonged to a certain social class, professional group, or religious confession. I was as ill at ease among artists and intellectuals as in bourgeois life, and it was a very long time since I had felt able to make personal friendships. No sooner did I become acquainted with someone than I feared I had come too close, no sooner did someone turn towards me than I began to retreat. In the end I was linked to other people only by certain forms of courtesy which I took to extremes and which I know today, said Austerlitz, I observed not so much for the sake of their recipients as because they allowed me to ignore the fact that my life has always, for as far back as I can remember, been clouded by unrelieved despair. It was then, after my work of destruction in the garden and when I had turned out my house, that I began my nocturnal wanderings through London, to escape the insomnia which increasingly tormented me. For over a year, I think, said Austerlitz, I would leave my house as darkness fell, walking on and on, down the Mile End Road and Bow Road to Stratford, then to Chigwell and Romford, right across Bethnal Green and Canonbury, through Holloway and Kentish Town and thus to Hampstead Heath, or else south over the river to Peckham and Dulwich or westward to Richmond Park. It is a fact that you can traverse this vast city almost from end to end on foot in a single night, said Austerlitz, and once you are used to walking alone and meeting only a few nocturnal spectres on your way, you soon begin to wonder why, apparently because of some agreement concluded long ago, Londoners of all ages lie in their beds in those countless buildings in

Greenwich, Bayswater or Kensington, under a safe roof, as they suppose, while really they are only stretched out with their faces turned to the earth in fear, like travellers of the past resting on their way through the desert. My wanderings took me to the most remote areas of London, into outlying parts of the metropolis which I would never otherwise have seen, and when dawn came I would go back to Whitechapel on the Underground, together with all the other poor souls who flow from the suburbs towards the centre at that time of day. As I passed through the stations, I thought several times that among the passengers coming towards me in the tiled passages, on the escalators plunging steeply into the depths, or behind the grey windows of a train just pulling out, I saw a face known to me from some much earlier part of my life, but I could never say whose it was. These familiar faces always had something different from the rest about them, something I might almost call indistinct, and on occasion they would haunt and disturb me for days on end. In fact at this time, usually when I came home from my nocturnal excursions, I began seeing what might be described as shapes and colours of diminished corporeality through a drifting veil or cloud of smoke, images from a faded world: a squadron of yachts putting out into the shadows over the sea from the glittering Thames estuary in the evening light, a horse-drawn cab in Spitalfields driven by a man in a top hat, a woman wearing the costume of the 1930s and casting her eyes down as she passed me by. It was at moments of particular weakness, when I thought I could not go on any longer, that my senses played these tricks on me. It sometimes seemed to me as if the noises of the city were dying down around me and the traffic was flowing silently down the street, or as if someone had plucked me by the sleeve. And I would hear people behind my back speaking in a foreign tongue, Lithuanian, Hungarian, or something else with a very alien note to it, or so I thought, said Austerlitz. I had several such experiences in Liverpool Street station, to which I was always irresistibly drawn back on my night journeys. Before work began to rebuild it at the end of the 1980s this station, with its main concourse fifteen to twenty feet below street level, was one of the darkest and most sinister places in London, a kind of entrance to the underworld, as it has often been described. The ballast between the tracks, the cracked sleepers, the brick walls with their stone bases, the cornices and panes of the tall windows, the wooden kiosks for the ticket inspectors, and the towering cast-iron columns with their palmate capitals were all covered in a greasy black layer formed, over the course of a century, by coke dust and soot, steam, sulphur and diesel oil. Even on sunny days only a faint greyness, scarcely illuminated at all by the globes of the station lights, came through the glass roof over the main hall, and in

this eternal dusk, which was full of a muffled babble of voices, a quiet scraping and trampling of feet, innumerable people passed in great tides, disembarking from the trains or boarding them, coming together, moving apart, and being held up at barriers and bottlenecks like water against a weir. Whenever I got out at Liverpool Street station on my way back to the East End, said Austerlitz, I would stay there at least a couple of hours, sitting on a bench with other passengers who were already tired in the early morning, or standing somewhere, leaning on a handrail and feeling that constant wrenching inside me, a kind of heartache which, as I was beginning to sense, was caused by the vortex of past time. I knew that on the site where the station stood marshy meadows had once extended to the city walls, meadows which froze over for months on end in the cold winters of the so-called Little Ice Age, and that Londoners used to strap bone runners under their shoes, skating there as the people of Antwerp skated on the Schelde, some-times going on until midnight in the flickering light of the bonfires burning here and there on the ice in heavy braziers. Later on, the marshes were pro-gressively drained, elm trees were planted, market gardens, fish ponds and white sandy paths were laid out to make a place where the citizens could walk in their leisure time, and soon pavilions and country houses were being built all the way out to Forest Park and Arden. Until the seventeenth century, Austerlitz continued, the priory of the order of St Mary of Bethlehem stood on the site of the present main station concourse and the Great Eastern Hotel. It had been founded by a certain Simon FitzMary in gratitude for his miraculous rescue from the hands of the Saracens when he was on a crusade, so that the pious brothers and sisters could pray henceforward for the salvation of the founder's soul and the souls of his ancestors, his descendants and all those related to him. The hospital for the insane and other destitute persons which has gone down in history under the name of Bedlam also belonged to the priory outside Bishopsgate. Whenever I was in the station, said Austerlitz, I kept almost obsessively trying to imagine – through the ever-changing maze of walls – the location in that huge space of the rooms where the asylum inmates were confined, and I often wondered whether the pain and suffering accumulated on this site over the centuries had ever really ebbed away, or whether they might not still, as I sometimes thought when I felt a cold breath of air on my forehead, be sensed as we pass through them on our way through the station halls and up and down the flights of steps. Or I imagined the bleachfields stretching westwards from Bedlam, saw the white lengths of linen spread out on the green grass and the diminutive figures of weavers and washerwomen, and on the far side of the bleachfields the places where the dead were buried once the churchyards of London could hold no more. When space becomes too cramped the dead, like the living, move out into less densely populated districts where they can rest at a decent distance from each other. But more and more keep coming, a never-ending succession of them, and in the end, when the space is entirely occupied, graves are dug through existing graves to accommodate them, until all the bones in the cemetery lie jumbled up together. At Broad Street station, built in 1865 on the site of the former burial grounds and bleachfields, excavations during the demolition work of 1984 brought to light over four hundred skeletons underneath a taxi rank. I went there quite often at the time, said Austerlitz, partly because of my interest in architectural history and partly for other reasons which I could not explain even to myself, and I took photographs of the remains of the dead. I remember falling into conversation with one of the archaeologists, who told me that on average the skeletons of eight people had been found in every cubic metre of earth removed from the trench. In the course of the seventeenth and

eighteenth centuries the city had grown above these strata of soil mingled with the dust and bones of decayed bodies into a warren of putrid streets and houses for the poorest Londoners, cobbled together out of beams, clods of clay, and any other building material that came to hand. Around 1860 and 1870, before work on the construction of the two north-east terminals began, these poverty-stricken quarters were forcibly cleared and vast quantities of soil, together with the bones buried in them, were dug up and removed, so that the railway lines, which on the engineers' plans looked like muscles and sinews in an anatomical atlas, could be brought to the outskirts of the City. Soon the site in front of Bishopsgate was nothing but a grey-brown morass, a no-man's-land where not a living soul stirred. The little river Wellbrook, the ditches and ponds, the crakes and snipe and herons, the elms and mulberry trees, Paul Pindar's deer park, the inmates of Bedlam and the starving paupers of Angel Alley, Peter Street, Sweet Apple Court and Swan Yard had all gone, and gone now too are the millions and millions of people who passed through Broadgate and Liverpool Street stations

day in, day out, for an entire century. As for me, said Austerlitz, I felt at this time as if the dead were returning from their exile and filling the twilight around me with their strangely slow but incessant to-ing and fro-ing. I remember, for instance, that one quiet Sunday morning I was sitting on a bench on the particularly gloomy platform where the boat trains from Harwich came in, watching a man who wore a snow-white turban with his shabby porter's uniform as he wielded a broom, sweeping up the rubbish scattered on the paving. In doing this job, which in its pointlessness reminded me of the eternal punishments that we are told, said Austerlitz, we must endure after death, the white-turbanned porter, oblivious of all around, per-formed the same movements over and over again using, instead of a proper dustpan, a cardboard box with one side removed, and nudging it along in front of him with his foot, first up the platform and then down again until he had returned to his point of departure, a low doorway in the builders' fence reaching up to the second storey of the inte-rior façade of the station. He had emerged from this doorway half an hour ago and now disappeared through it again, with an odd jerk, as it seemed to me. To this day I cannot explain what made me follow him, said Austerlitz. We take almost all the decisive steps in our lives as a result of slight inner adjustments of which we are barely conscious. But in any case, that Sunday morning I suddenly found myself on the other side of the tall fence, facing the entrance to the Ladies' Waiting-Room, the existence of which, in this remote part of the station, had been quite unknown to me. The man in the turban was nowhere to be seen, and there was no one on the scaffolding either. I hesitated to approach the swing doors, but as soon as I had taken hold of the brass handle I stepped past a heavy curtain hung on the inside to keep out draughts, and entered the large room, which had obviously been disused for years. I felt, said Austerlitz, like an actor who, upon making his entrance, has completely and irrevocably forgotten not only the lines he knew by heart but the very part he has so often played. Minutes or even hours may have passed while I stood in that empty space beneath a ceiling which seemed to float at a vertiginous height, unable to move from the spot, with my face raised to the icy grey light, like moonshine, which came through the windows in a crossing deep chasms thronged with tiny figures who looked to me, said Austerlitz, like prisoners in search of some way of escape from their dungeon, and the longer I stared upwards with my head wrenched painfully back, the more I felt as if the room where I stood were expanding, going on for ever and ever in an improbably foreshortened perspective, at the same time turning back into itself in a way possible only in such a deranged universe. Once I thought that very far away I saw a dome of open-work masonry, with a parapet around it on which grew ferns, young willows and various other shrubs where herons had built their large, untidy nests, and I saw the birds spread their great wings and fly away through the blue air. I remember, said Austerlitz, that in the middle of this vision of imprisonment and liberation I could not stop wondering whether it was a ruin or a building in the process of construction that I had entered. Both ideas were right in a way at the time, since the new station was literally rising from the ruins of the old Liverpool Street; in any case, the crucial point was hardly this speculation in itself, which was really only a distraction, but the scraps of memory beginning to drift through the outlying regions of my mind: images, for instance, like the recollection of a late November afternoon in 1968 when I stood with Marie de Verneuil – whom I had met in Paris, and of whom I shall have more to say – when we stood in the nave of the wonderful church of Salle in Norfolk, which towers in isolation above the wide fields, and I could not bring out the words I should have spoken then. White mist had risen from the meadows outside, and we watched in silence as it crept slowly into the church porch, a rippling vapour rolling forward at ground level and gradually spreading over the entire stone floor, becoming denser and denser and rising visibly higher, until we ourselves emerged from it only above the waist and it seemed about to stifle us. Memories like this came back to me in the disused Ladies' Waiting-Room of Liverpool Street station, memories behind and within which many things much further back in the past seemed to lie, all interlocking like the labyrinthine vaults I saw in the dusty grey light, and which seemed to go on and on for ever. In fact I felt, said Austerlitz, that the waiting-room where I stood as if dazzled contained all the hours of my past life, all the suppressed and extinguished fears sense of shame and sorrow, or perhaps something quite different, something inexpressible because we have no words for it, just as I had no words all those years ago when the two strangers came over to me speaking a language I did not understand. All I do know is that when I saw the boy sitting on the bench I became aware, through my dull bemusement, of the destructive effect on me of my desolation through all those past years, and a terrible weariness overcame me at the idea that I had never really been alive, or was only now being born, almost on the eve of my death. I can only guess what reasons may have induced the minister Elias and his wan wife to take me to live with them in the summer of 1939, said Austerlitz. Childless as they were, perhaps they hoped to reverse the petrifaction of their emotions, which must have been becoming more unbearable to them every day, by devoting themselves together to bringing up a boy then aged four and a half, or perhaps they thought they owed it to a higher authority to perform some good work beyond the level of ordinary charity, a work entailing personal devotion and sacrifice. Or perhaps they thought they ought to save my soul, innocent as it was of the Christian faith. I myself cannot say what my first few days in Bala with the Eliases really felt like. I do remember new clothes which made me very unhappy, and the inexplicable disappearance of my little green rucksack, and recently I have even thought that I could still apprehend the dying away of my native tongue, the faltering and fading sounds which I think lingered on in me at least for a while, like something shut up and scratching or knocking, something which, out of fear, stops its noise and falls silent whenever one tries to listen to it. And certainly the words I had forgotten in a short space of time, and all that went with them, would have remained buried in the depths of my mind had I not, through a series of coincidences, entered the old waiting-room in Liverpool Street station that Sunday morning, a few weeks at the most before it vanished for ever in the rebuilding. I have no idea how long I stood in the waiting-room, said Austerlitz, nor how I got out again and which way I walked back, through Bethnal Green or Stepney, reaching home at last as dark began to fall. Exhausted as I was, I lay down in my drenched clothes and fell into a deep, uneasy sleep from which, as I discovered afterwards by making the through the faint light of dawn. In the middle of these dreams, said Austerlitz, somewhere behind his eyes, he had felt these overwhelmingly immediate images forcing their way out of him, but once he had woken he could recall scarcely any of them even in outline. I realized then, he said, how little practice I had in using my memory, and conversely how hard I must always have tried to recollect as little as possible, avoiding everything which related in any way to my unknown past. Inconceivable as it seems to me today, I knew nothing about the conquest of Europe by the Germans and the slave state they set up, and nothing about the persecution I had escaped, or at least, what I did know was not much more than a salesgirl in a shop, for instance, knows about the plague or cholera. As far as I was concerned the world ended in the late nineteenth century. I dared go no further than that, although in fact the whole history of the architecture and civilization of the bourgeois age, the subject of my research, pointed in the direction of the catastrophic events already casting their shadows before them at the time. I did not read newspapers because, as I now know, I feared unwelcome revelations, I turned on the radio only at certain hours of the day, I was always refining my defensive reactions, creating a kind of quarantine or immune system which, as I maintained my existence in a smaller and smaller space, protected me from anything that could be connected in any way, however distant, with my own early history. Moreover, I had constantly been preoccupied by that accumulation of knowledge which I had pursued for decades, and which served as a substitute or compensatory memory. And if some dangerous piece of information came my way despite all my precautions, as it inevitably did, I was clearly capable of closing my eyes and ears to it, of simply forgetting it like any other unpleasantness. Yet this self-censorship of my mind, the constant suppression of the memories surfacing in me, Austerlitz continued, demanded ever greater efforts and finally, and unavoidably, led to the almost total paralysis of my linguistic faculties, the destruction of all my notes and sketches, my endless nocturnal peregrinations through London, and the hallucinations which plagued me with increasing frequency up to the point of my nervous breakdown in the summer of 1992. I cannot say exactly how I spent the rest of that year, said Austerlitz; all I know is that next spring, when there was some improvement in my state of health, on one of my first ventures into the city I visited an antiquarian bookshop near the British Museum where I regularly went in search of architectural engravings. Absent-mindedly, I leafed through the various boxes and drawers, staring sometimes for minutes on end at a star-shaped vault or diamond frieze, a hermitage, a monopteros or a mausoleum, without knowing what I was looking at or why. The owner of the bookshop, Penelope Peacefull, a very beautiful woman whom I had admired for many years, was sitting where she always sat in the mornings, slightly to one side of her desk with its load of books and papers, solving the crossword puzzle on the back of the *Telegraph* with her left hand. She smiled at me from time to time and then looked out at the street again, deep in thought. It was quiet in the shop except for soft voices coming from the little radio which stood beside Penelope, as usual, and these voices, which at first I could hardly make out but which soon became almost too distinct, cast such a spell over me that I entirely forgot the engravings lying before me, and stood there as still as if on no account must I let a single

on the grid. When we had parted I sat for an hour on a bench in Russell Square under the tall plane trees, which were still leafless. It was a sunny day. A number of starlings were marching up and down on the grass, pecking desultorily at the crocuses. I watched them, noticing how the green-gold hues in their dark plumage gleamed, depending which way they turned to catch the light, and came to the conclusion that although I did not know whether I had come to England on the *Prague* or on some other ferry, the mere mention of the city's name in the present context was enough to convince me that I would have to go there. I thought of the difficulties Hilary had encountered when, during my last months at Stower Grange, he began taking steps to have me naturalized, and how he had never been able to find out anything from any of the social-services offices in Wales, or the Foreign Office, or the Aid Committee under whose auspices the transports of refugee children had come to England and who had lost a number of files during their several moves and evacuations, carried out during the bombing of London in very difficult circumstances and almost entirely without trained staff. I got the addresses of authorities who might be consulted in a case like mine from the embassy of the Czech Republic, and then, immediately after arriving at Ruzyně airport on a day which was much too bright, almost over-exposed, a day, said Austerlitz, when people looked as ill and grey as if they were all chronic smokers not far from death, I took a taxi to the Karmelitská in the Lesser Quarter, where the state archives are housed in a very peculiar building going far back in time if not even, like so much in the city of Prague, standing outside time altogether. You go in through a narrow doorway let into the main

portal, and find yourself first in a dim barrel-vaulted entrance through which coaches and carriages used to drive into the inner courtyard. This courtyard measures some twenty by fifty metres, is roofed by a glazed dome, and on three storeys has galleries running round it, giving access to

the rooms containing the archives, where the windows look out on the street. The entire building, from the outside more like a mansion house than anything else, therefore consists of four wings, each not much more than three metres deep, set around the courtyard in an almost Illusionist manner and without any corridors or passages in them. It is a style resembling the prison architecture of the bourgeois epoch, when it was decided that the most useful design for the penal system was to build wings of cells around a rectangular or circular courtyard, with catwalks running along the interior. And it was not just of a prison that the archives building in the Karmelitská reminded me, said Austerlitz; it also suggested a monastery, a riding school, an opera house and a lunatic asylum, and all these ideas mingled in my mind as I looked at the twilight coming in from above, and thought that on the rows of galleries I saw a dense crowd of people, some of them waving hats or handkerchiefs, as passengers on board a steamer used to do when it put out to sea. At any rate, it was a little while before I managed to bring myself back to the present, and turned to the lodge near the entrance, from which the porter had been keeping an eye on me ever since I had crossed the threshold and, attracted by the light of the interior courtyard, had passed by him without noticing his presence. If you wanted to speak to this porter you had to lean a long way down to his window, which was so low that he appeared to be kneeling on the floor of his lodge. Although I had soon adopted the right position, said Austerlitz, I could not make myself understood, with the result that after launching into a long verbal torrent in which I could make out nothing but the words *anglický* and *Angličan*, repeated several times with special emphasis, the porter eventually phoned to request assistance from one of the archive's officials, who did indeed, at practically the next moment, while I was still filling in a visitor's form at the desk opposite the

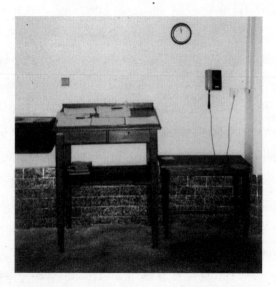

lodge, materialize beside me as if she had, as they say, sprung out of the ground. Tereza Ambrosová – so she introduced herself to me, immediately asking in her slightly hesitant but otherwise very correct English what I wanted to know – Tereza Ambrosová was a pale woman of almost transparent appearance, mountains of paper, in plain clay flowerpots or brightly coloured majolica jardinières: mimosas and myrtles, thick-leaved aloes, gardenias, and a large hoya twining its way around a trelliswork frame. Mrs Ambrosová, who had very courteously pulled out a chair for me beside her desk, listened attentively with her head tilted slightly to one side as, for the first time in my life, I began explaining to someone else that because of certain circumstances my origins had been unknown to me, and for other reasons I had never inquired into them, but now felt compelled, because of a series of coincidental events, to conclude or at least to conjecture that I had left Prague at the age of four and a half, in the months just before the war broke out, on one of the so-called children's transports departing from the city at the time, and I had therefore come to consult the archives in the hope that people of my surname living here between 1934 and 1939, who could not have been very numerous, might be found in the registers, with details of their addresses. I fell into such a panic as I offered these explanations, which suddenly struck me as not just far too cursory but positively absurd, that I began to stammer and could hardly bring out a word. All at once I felt the heat from the stout radiator, which was encrusted with several layers of lumpy oil paint and stood under the wide-open window; I heard nothing but the noise rising from the Karmelitská, the heavy rumble of the trams, the wailing sirens of police cars and ambulances somewhere in the distance, and I calmed down only when Tereza Ambrosová, whose deep-set violet eyes had been gazing at me with some concern, gave me a glass of water. As I took a few sips from this glass, which I had to hold in both hands, she said that the registers of those living in Prague at the time in question had been preserved complete, that Austerlitz was indeed one of the more unusual surnames, so she thought there could be no particular difficulty in finding me the entries I wanted by tomorrow afternoon. She would see to it personally, she told me. I cannot remember, said Austerlitz, with what words I said goodbye to Mrs Ambrosová, how I got out of the archives building or where I went after that; all I know is that I took a room in a small hotel on Kampa Island not far from the Karmelitská and sat there by the window until darkness fell, looking out at the heavy, leaden grey waters of the Vltava, and over the river to the city, which I now feared was entirely alien to me, a place

The names were followed by the professions of their bearers – dealer in textiles *en gros*, rabbi, bandages manufacturer, principal clerk, silversmith, printing works proprietor, and finally opera singer – together with the number of the city district and the street: VII U vozovky, II Betlemská, and so on. Mrs Ambrosová suggested that before crossing the river I might begin my inquiries in the Lesser Quarter, which wasn't ten minutes' walk away from here, she said. I could try the Šporkova, a small street a few paces uphill from the Schönborn Palace, where the register of inhabitants for 1938 said that Agáta Austerlitzová had been living at Number Twelve in that year. And so, said Austerlitz, no sooner had I arrived in Prague than I found myself back among the scenes of my early childhood, every trace of which had been expunged from my memory for as long as I could recollect. As I walked through the labyrinth of alleyways, thoroughfares and courtyards between the Vlašská and Nerudova, and still more so when I felt the uneven paving of the Šporkova underfoot as step by step I climbed uphill, it was as if I had already been this way before and memories were revealing themselves to me not by means of any mental effort but through my senses, so long numbed and now coming back to life. It was true that I could recognize nothing for certain, yet I had to keep stopping now and then because my glance was caught by a finely wrought window grating, the iron handle of a bell-pull, or the branches of an almond tree growing over a garden wall. Once I stood for a considerable time outside the vaulted entrance to a building, said Austerlitz, looking up at a half-relief set in the smooth plaster above the keystone of the arch. The cast was no more than a square foot in size, and showed, set against a spangled sea-green back-ground, a blue dog carrying a small branch in its mouth, which I could tell, by the prickling of my scalp, it had brought back out of my past. Then there was the cool air as I entered the front hall of Number Twelve Šporkova, the metal box for the electrics built into the wall beside the entrance with its light-ning symbol, the octofoil mosaic flower in shades of

dove grey and snow white set in the flecked
artificial-stone floor of the hall, the smell of damp
limewash, the gently rising flight of stairs, with

hazelnut-shaped iron knobs placed at intervals in
the handrail of the banisters – all of them signs and
characters from the type-case of forgotten things, I

thought, and was overcome by such a state of blissful yet anxious confusion that more than once I had to sit down on the steps in the quiet stairwell and lean my head against the wall. It may have been as much as an hour before I finally rang the bell of the right-hand flat on the top floor, and then half an eternity seemed to pass before I heard movement inside, the door was opened, and I found myself facing Vera Ryšanová, who – as she was soon to tell me – had been my mother Agáta's neighbour and my nurserymaid in the thirties when she, Vera, had been studying Romance languages at Prague University. I think that the reason why I did not immediately recognize her, said Austerlitz, although despite her fragility she seemed quite unchanged, was my agitated condition, in which I could hardly believe my eyes. So I merely stammered out the sentence I had laboriously learnt by heart the day before: *Prominte, prosím, že Vás obtěžuji. Hledám paní Agátu Austerlitzovou, která zde možná v roce devatenáct set třicet osm bydlela*. I am looking for a Mrs Agáta Austerlitzová who may have been living here in 1938. With a gesture of alarm, Vera covered her face with both hands, hands which, it flashed through my mind, were endlessly familiar to me, stared at

throughout Europe, a kind of second Switzerland, while Agáta's rather more colourful notion of the ideal world was inspired by the works of Jacques Offenbach, whom she admired enormously, which incidentally, said Vera, was the reason for my first name, not a usual one among Czechs. It was through an interest in every aspect of French civilization, she added, something which as an enthusiastic student of Romance culture I shared with both Agáta and Maximilian, that a friendship began to develop between us immediately after our first conversation on the day when they moved in, a friendship which led as if quite naturally, so Vera told me, said Austerlitz, to her offering, since unlike Agáta and Maximilian she had her time largely at her own disposal, to assume the duties of nanny for the few years until I started nursery school. It was an offer she had never once regretted later, said Vera, for even before I could talk it had always seemed to her as if no one understood her better than this small boy who, by the age of not quite three, entertained her in the most delightful way with his conversational gifts. By agreement with Agáta, when we walked over the meadow slopes of the Seminar Garden among the pear and cherry trees,

or on hot days through the shadier grounds of the
park of Schönborn Palace, we spoke French, and
only when we came home late in the afternoon and
Vera was making our supper did we revert to
Czech, for the discussion of more domestic and
childish matters, as it were. In the middle of her
account Vera herself, quite involuntarily, had
changed from one language to the other, and I, who
had not for a moment thought that Czech could
mean anything to me, not at the airport or in the
state archives, or even while learning by heart
the question which would have been of scant use to
me addressed to the wrong quarters, now understood almost everything Vera said, like a deaf man
whose hearing has been miraculously restored, so
that all I wanted to do was close my eyes and listen
for ever to her polysyllabic flood of words. In the
warm season of the year in particular, said Vera, she
had always had to move the geraniums on the sill
aside as soon as we came back from our daily walk,
so that I could take my favourite place on the
window-seat and look down on the garden with its
lilac trees and the low building opposite where the
hunchbacked tailor Moravec had his workshop, and
while she, so Vera said, cut bread and boiled the

kettle, I used to give her a running commentary on whatever Moravec happened to be doing: mending the worn hem of a jacket, rummaging in his button box, or sewing a quilted lining into an overcoat. But I was particularly anxious, Vera told me, said Austerlitz, not to miss the moment when Moravec put down his needle and thread, his big scissors and the other tools of his trade, cleared the baize-covered table, spread a double sheet of newspaper on it, and laid out on this sheet blackened with print the supper he must have been looking forward to for some time, a supper which varied according to the season and might be curd cheese with chives, a long radish, a few tomatoes with onions, a smoked herring or boiled potatoes. He's putting the sleeve dummy in the wardrobe, he's going out into the kitchen, now he's bringing in his beer, now he's sharpening his knife, he's cutting a slice of sausage, taking a long drink from his glass, wiping the foam from his mouth with the back of his hand — it was in this or some similar fashion, always the same yet always slightly different, that I used to describe the tailor's supper to her almost every evening, said Vera, and I often had to be reminded not to forget my own bread-and-butter soldiers. As she told me about my curious love of such observations, Vera had risen and opened both the inner and the outer windows to let me look down into the garden next door, where the lilac happened to be in flower, its blossoms so thick and white that in the gathering dusk it looked as if there had been a snow-storm in the middle of spring. And the sweet fragrance wafting up from the walled garden, the waxing moon already in the sky above the rooftops, the sound of church bells ringing down in the city, and the yellow façade of the tailor's house with its green balcony where Moravec, who as Vera told me had died long ago, frequently used to be seen in his time, swinging his heavy iron filled with red-hot coals through the air, these and other images, said Austerlitz, ranged themselves side by side, so that deeply buried and locked away within me as they had been, they now came luminously back to my mind as I looked out of the window. It was the same when Vera, without a word, opened the door to the room where the little couch on which I always slept when my parents were away still stood in its place, at the foot of the four-poster bed with its barley-sugar uprights and pillows piled high which, together with the rest of the furniture, she had inherited from her great-aunt. The crescent moon shone into the dark room, and there was a white blouse hanging from the catch of the half-open window just as it had always hung there in the past, I now remembered, said Austerlitz. I saw Vera as she had been then, sitting beside me on the divan telling me stories from the Riesengebirge and the Bohemian Forest, I saw her uncommonly beautiful eyes misting over in the twilight, so to speak, when after reaching the end of the story she took off her glasses and bent down to me. Later, I now remembered, while she sat in the next room over her books, I liked to lie awake for a while, safe as I knew myself to be in the care of my solicitous guardian and the pale glow of the circle of light where she sat reading. With only the slightest effort of will I could conjure it all up; the hunchbacked tailor, who would now be in his own bedchamber, the moon travelling round the building, the patterns of the carpet and wallpaper, even the course traced by the hairline cracks in the tiles of the tall stove. But when I got tired of this game and wanted to go to sleep I had only to wait to hear Vera lift the next leaf of her book in the other room, and I can still feel, said Austerlitz, or perhaps it is only now that I feel again, the sense of my consciousness dissolving among the poppies and leafy tendrils etched into the opaque glass of the door before I caught the slight rustle of the page turning. On our walks, Vera continued when we were sitting in the living-room again, and she had given me a cup of peppermint tea with her two now unsteady hands, on our walks we hardly ever went further than the Seminar Garden, the Khotek Gardens and the other green spaces in the Lesser Quarter. Only occasionally, in summer, did we make rather longer expeditions with my little pushchair, which as I might perhaps remember had a small coloured whirligig fastened to it, going as far as Sofia Island, the swimming school on the banks of the Vltava, or the observation platform on Petřín Hill, from which we may have spent an hour or more looking at the city spread out below us with its many towers, all of which I had known by heart, as well as the names of the seven bridges spanning the glittering river. Since I have been unable to go out of doors, so that I now see almost nothing new, said Vera, the pictures we enjoyed so much at the time come back to me with increasing clarity, like pure fantasies. I often feel, said Vera, as if I were gazing at a diorama upwards like a fat caterpillar, while further out, on the other side of the city, the railway train you always waited so eagerly to see is making its way past the row of houses at the foot of the Vyšehrad and slowly crossing the bridge over the river, trailing a white cloud of vapour. When the weather was bad, said Vera, we often visited my aunt Otýlie in the glove shop on the Šeríková which she had been running since before the Great War and in which, as in some consecrated shrine or temple, a muted atmosphere banishing all profane ideas reigned. Aunt Otýlie was a spinster lady of alarmingly fragile appearance. She always wore an outer garment of pleated black silk with a detachable white lace collar, and moved about in a little cloud of lily-of-the-valley perfume. If she was not busy serving one of the women she described as her honoured lady clients, she was constantly occupied in maintaining order among her stock of hundreds, if not thousands, of different pairs of gloves of all kinds, ranging from cotton for everyday wear to the most elegant velvet or kid creations from Paris and Milan, arranged in a hierarchy of her own devising which she had preserved for decades through all the vicissitudes of time, and which only she really first night, we went to the dress rehearsal of the operetta together, and as soon as we entered the theatre by the stage door, she said, I fell into a reverent silence, although I had been chattering nineteen to the dozen on our way through the city. I had also been unusually quiet and lost in thought during the performance of the somewhat haphazard arrangement of scenes, and on our way home by tram as well. It was because of this more or less casual remark of Vera's, said Austerlitz, that I went to see the Estates Theatre next morning, and sat alone for a long time in the stalls directly under the top of the dome, having obtained permission from the porter, in exchange for a not inconsiderable tip, to take some photographs in the recently refurbished auditorium. Around me the tiers of seats with their gilded adornments shining through the dim light rose to the roof; before me the proscenium arch of the stage on which Agáta had once stood was like a blind eye. And the harder I tried to conjure up at least some faint recollection of her appearance, the more the theatre seemed to be shrinking, as if I myself had shrunk to the stature of a little Tom Thumb enclosed in a sort of velvet-lined casket. Only after a while, when someone or bered that I had been filled by a grief previously unknown to me when, long past my usual bedtime, I lay with my eyes wide open in the dark on the divan in Vera's room, listening to the church clocks strike the quarter-hours and waiting for Agáta to come home, waiting to hear the car bringing her back from that other world stop outside the gate, waiting for her to come into the room at last and sit down beside me, enveloped by a strange theatrical odour in which dust and drifts of perfume mingled. I see her wearing an ashen-grey silk bodice laced up in front, but I cannot make out her face, only an iridescent veil of pale, cloudy milkiness wafting close to her skin, and then, said Austerlitz, I see the scarf slip from her right shoulder as she lays her hand on my forehead. On my third day in Prague, so Austerlitz continued his story, when he had recovered some degree of composure, I went up to the Seminar Garden early in the morning. The cherry and pear trees of Vera's story had now been grubbed up and replaced by young saplings, with thin branches which would not bear fruit for some time yet to come. The path wound uphill, describ-ing wide curves through the grass, which was wet with dew. Halfway up I met an old lady with an overfed, reddish-brown dachshund which was not very good on its legs and stopped now and then, staring with its brow furrowed at the ground ahead of it. The sight of it reminded me that on my walks with Vera I often used to see old ladies of this kind with bad-tempered little dogs, almost always wearing wire muzzles, which may have been the reason for their mute ill-will. Then I sat on a bench in the sun until nearly midday, looking out over the buildings of the Lesser Quarter and the River Vltava at the panorama of the city, which seemed to be veined with the curving cracks and rifts of past time, like the varnish on a painting. A little later, said Austerlitz, I discovered another such pattern created by no discernible law in the

entwined roots of a chestnut tree clinging to a steep slope, through which Vera had told me, said Austerlitz, I liked to climb as a child. And the dark-green yews growing under the taller trees were familiar to me too, as familiar as the cool air which enveloped me at the bottom of the ravine and the countless windflowers covering the woodland floor, faded now in April, and I understood why, on one of my visits to a Gloucestershire country house with Hilary years ago, my voice failed me when, in the park which was laid out very much like the Schönborn gardens, we unexpectedly came upon a north-facing slope covered by the finely cut leaves and snow-white blooms of the March-flowering *Anemone nemorosa*.

— It was with the botanical name of these shade-loving anemones that Austerlitz concluded another section of his story on that evening in the late winter of 1997, when we sat in the Alderney Street house amidst what seemed to me a silence of unfathomable profundity. Quarter or half an hour may have gone by in the light of the blue, evenly flickering flames of the little gas fire, before Austerlitz rose and said it would probably be best if I spent the night under his roof. So saying, he went upstairs ahead of me, and led me into a room which, like those on the ground floor, was quite unfurnished except for a kind of camp bed standing unfolded against one wall, with handles at both ends so that it resembled a stretcher. Beside the bed there was a wine crate with a blackened coat of arms burnt into it which had once contained Château Gruaud-Larose, and on the crate, in the gentle light of a shaded lamp, stood a glass, a carafe of water, and an old-fashioned radio in a dark-brown Bakelite case. Austerlitz wished me good night and latched the door carefully behind him. I went over to the window, looked down at the empty street below, turned back to the room, sat down on the bed, undid my shoelaces, thought about Austerlitz, whom I could now hear moving about the room next door, and then, when I looked up again, saw in the faint light a small collection of seven variously shaped Bakelite jars on the mantelpiece. None of these containers was more than two or three inches high, and when I opened them one by one and held them in the light of the lamp, each proved to contain the mortal remains of one of the moths which – as Austerlitz had told me – had met its end here in this house. I tipped one of them, a weightless, ivory-coloured creature with folded wings that might have been woven of some immaterial fabric, out of its Bakelite box on to the palm of my right hand. Its legs, which it had drawn up under its silver-scaled body as if just clearing some final obstacle, were so delicate that I could scarcely make them out, while the antennae curving high above the whole body also trembled on the edge of visibility. However, the staring black eye projecting somewhat from the head was distinct enough. Spellbound by this nocturnal apparition, which although it might have died years ago bore no sign of decay, I studied it intently before replacing it in its narrow tomb. As I lay down I turned on the radio set standing on the wine crate beside the bed. The names of cities and radio stations with which I used to link the most exotic ideas in my

disposition which he shared with Agáta, had been convinced ever since I knew him, said Vera, so Austerlitz told me, that the parvenus who had come to power in Germany and the corporate bodies and other human swarms endlessly proliferating under the new regime, a spectacle which inspired him, as he often said, with a sense of positive horror, had abandoned themselves from the first to a blind lust for conquest and destruction, taking its cue from the magic word thousand which the Reichskanzler, as we could all hear on the wireless, repeated constantly in his speeches. A thousand, ten thousand, twenty thousand, thirty-seven thousand, two hundred and forty thousand, a thousand times a thousand, thousands upon thousands: such was the refrain he barked out in his hoarse voice, drumming into the Germans the notion that the promise of their own greatness was about to be fulfilled. None the less, said Vera, Austerlitz continued, Maximilian did not in any way believe that the German people had been driven into their misfortune; rather, in his view, they had entirely re-created themselves in this perverse form, engendered by every individual's wishful thinking and bound up with false family sentiment, and had then brought forth, as symbolic exponents of their innermost desires, so to speak, the Nazi grandees, whom Maximilian regarded without exception as muddle-headed and indolent. From time to time, so Vera recollected, said Austerlitz, Maximilian would tell the tale of how once, after a trade-union meeting in Teplitz in the early summer of 1933, he had gone a little way up into the Erzgebirge, where he came upon some day-trippers in a beer garden who had been buying all manner of things in a village on the German side of the border, including a new kind of boiled sweet which had, embedded in its sugary mass, a raspberry-coloured swastika that literally melted in the mouth. At the sight of these Nazi treats, Maximilian had said, he suddenly realized that the Germans had wholly reorganized their production lines, from heavy industry down to the manufacturing of items such as these vulgar sweets, not because they had been ordered to do so but each of his own accord, out of enthusiasm for the national resurgence. Vera went on, said Austerlitz, to tell me that Maximilian visited Austria and Germany several times in the 1930s, to gain a more accurate idea of general developments, and that she remembered precisely how, immediately after returning from

Nuremberg, he had described the Führer's prodigious reception at the Party rally. Hours before his arrival, the entire population of Nuremberg and indeed people from much further afield, crowds flocking in not just from Franconia and Bavaria but from the most remote parts of the country, Holstein and Pomerania, Silesia and the Black Forest, stood shoulder to shoulder all agog with excitement along the predetermined route, until at last, heralded by roars of acclamation, the motorcade of heavy Mercedes limousines came gliding at walking pace down the narrow alley which parted the sea of radiant uplifted faces and the arms outstretched in yearning. Maximilian had told her, said Vera, that in the middle of this crowd, which had merged into a single living organism racked by strange, convulsive contractions, he had felt like a foreign body about to be crushed and then excreted. From where he stood in the square outside the Lorenzkirche, he said, he saw the motorcade making its slow way through the swaying masses down to the Old Town, where the houses with their pointed and crooked gables, their occupants hanging out of the windows like bunches of grapes, resembled a hopelessly overcrowded ghetto into which, so Maximilian had said, the long-awaited saviour was now making his entry. It was in just the same vein, said Vera, that Maximilian later repeatedly described the spectacular film of the Party rally which he had seen in a Munich cinema, and which confirmed his suspicions that, out of the humiliation from which the Germans had never recovered, they were now developing an image of themselves as a people chosen to evangelize the world. Not only did the overawed spectators witness the Führer's aeroplane descending slowly to earth through towering mountain ranges of cloud; not only was the tragic history they all shared invoked in the ceremony honouring the war dead during which, as Maximilian described it to us, Hitler and Höss and Himmler strode down the broad avenue lined, in straight serried ranks, with columns and companies created by the power of the new state out of a host of immovable German bodies, to the accompaniment of a funeral march which stirred the innermost soul of the entire nation; not only might one see warriors pledging themselves to die for the Fatherland, and the huge forests of flags mysteriously swaying as they moved away by torch-light into the dark — no, said Vera, Maximilian told us that a bird's-eye view showed a city of white tents extending to the horizon, from which as day broke the Germans emerged singly, in couples or in small groups, forming a silent procession and pressing ever closer together as they all went in the same direction, following, so it seemed, some higher bidding, on their way to the Promised Land at last after long years in the wilderness. It was only a few months after this experience of Maximilian's in the Munich cinema that the Austrians were to be heard over the wireless, hundreds of thousands of them pouring into the Heldenplatz in Vienna, their shouts breaking over us like a flood tide for hours on end, said Vera. In Maximilian's opinion, she told me, this collective paroxysm on the part of the Viennese crowds marked the watershed. It was still a sinister echo in our ears when, with summer hardly over, the first refugees arrived here in Prague, expelled from the now so-called Ostmark region after being robbed by their former fellow citizens of everything but a few schillings. In what they probably knew was the false hope of keeping their heads above water in a foreign country, they went from door to door as itinerant pedlars, offering for sale hairpins and slides, pencils and writing paper, ties and other items of haberdashery, just as their ancestors had

Vera, Maximilian stayed in Prague throughout the winter, whether because of his work for the Party, which was now a matter of particular urgency, or because he refused, for as long as was humanly possible, to give up his belief that the law would protect a man. For her part, Agáta was not prepared to go to France ahead of Maximilian, although he had repeatedly advised her to leave, and so it was that your father, Vera told me, said Austerlitz, then in the utmost danger, did not leave until it was almost too late, on the afternoon of the fourteenth of March, by plane from Ruzyně to Paris. I still remember, said Vera, that when he said goodbye he was wearing a wonderful plum-coloured double-breasted suit, and a black felt hat with a green band and a broad brim. Next morning, at first light, the Germans did indeed march into Prague in the middle of a heavy snowstorm which seemed to make them appear out of nowhere. When they crossed the bridge and their armoured cars were rolling up the Narodní a profound silence fell over the whole city. People turned away, and from that moment they walked more slowly, like somnambulists, as if they no longer knew where they were going. What particularly upset us, so Vera remarked, said Austerlitz, was the instant change to driving on the right. It often made my heart miss a beat, she said, when I saw a car racing down the road on the wrong side, since it inevitably made me think that from now on we must live in a world turned upside down. Of course, Vera continued, it was much harder for Agáta than for me to manage under the new regime. Since the Germans had issued their decrees on the Jewish population, she could go shopping only at certain times; she must not take a taxi, she could sit only in the last carriage of the tram, she could not visit a coffee-house or cinema, or attend a concert or any other event. Nor could she herself appear on stage any more, and access to the banks of the Vltava and the parks and gardens she had loved so much was barred to her. All my green places are lost to me, she once said, adding that only now did she truly understand how wonderful it is to stand by the rail of a river steamer without a care in the world. The ever-extended list of bans — before long it was forbidden for Jews to walk on the pavement on the side of the road next to the park, to go into a laundry or dry cleaner's, or to make a call from a public telephone — all of this, I still hear Vera telling me, said Austerlitz, soon brought Agáta to the brink of despair. I can see her now pacing up and down this room, said Vera, I can see her striking her forehead with the flat of her hand, and crying out, chanting the syllables one by one: I do not un der stand it! I do not un der stand it! I shall ne ver un der stand it!! None the less, she went into the city as often as she could, applying to I don't know how many or what authorities, she stood for hours in the sole post office which the forty thousand Jews in Prague were allowed to use, waiting to send a tele-gram; she made inquiries, pulled strings, left finan-cial deposits, produced affidavits and guarantees, and when she came home she would sit up racking her brains until late into the night. But the more trouble she took, and the longer she went on trying, the further did any hope of her getting an emigration permit recede, so in the summer, when there was already talk of the forthcoming war and the likeli-hood of even harsher restrictions when it broke out, she finally decided, Vera told me, said Austerlitz, that she would send me at least to England, having succeeded through the good offices of one of her theatrical friends in getting my name put down for one of the few children's transports leaving Prague for London during those months. Vera remem-bered, said Austerlitz, that the happy excitement

Agáta felt at this first successful outcome of her
efforts was overshadowed by her grief and anxiety as
she imagined how I would feel, a boy not yet five
years old who had always led a sheltered life, on my
long railway journey and then among strangers in a
foreign country. On the other hand, said Vera, Agáta
hoped that now the first step had been taken, some
way for her to leave too would surely be found quite
quickly, and then you could all be together in Paris.
So she was torn between wishful thinking and her
fear that she was doing something irresponsible and
unforgivable, and who knows, Vera said to me,
whether she might not have kept you with her after
all had there been just a few more days left before
you were to set off from Prague. I have only an
indistinct, rather blurred picture of the moment of
farewell at the Wilsonova station, said Vera, adding,
after a few moments' reflection, that I had my things
with me in a little leather suitcase, and food for the
journey in a rucksack — *un petit sac à dos avec quelques
viatiques*, said Austerlitz, those had been Vera's exact
words, summing up, as he now thought, the whole
of his later life. Vera also remembered the twelve-
year-old girl with the bandoneon to whose care they
had entrusted me, a Charlie Chaplin comic bought at

along the ceiling down which the lifeless bodies were pushed a little further as required. The bill for these cursory proceedings was sent to the relations of the hanged or guillotined victim, with the information that it could be settled in monthly instalments. Although little hint of it made its way out at the time, fear of the Germans spread through the whole city like a creeping miasma. Agáta said it even drifted in through the closed doors and windows, taking one's breath away. When I look back at the two years following the outbreak of the war, said Vera, it is as if at that time everything was caught in a vortex whirling downwards at ever-increasing speed. Bulletins came thick and fast over the wireless, read by the announcers in a curiously high-pitched tone of voice, as if forced out of the larynx: news of the never-ending exploits of the Wehrmacht, which had soon occupied the entire European continent, while its successive campaigns, with apparently conclusive logic, held out to the Germans the prospect of a vast world empire in which, thanks to the fact that they belonged to the chosen people, they would all be able to embark on the most glittering careers. I believe, Vera told me, said Austerlitz, that even the last remaining German sceptics were overcome by a records she loved so much, her binoculars and opera glasses, musical instruments, jewellery, furs and the clothes Maximilian had left behind to the so-called Compulsory Collection Centre. Because of some mistake she had made in complying with this order, she was sent to shovel snow on Ruzyně airfield on a freezing day – winter came very early that year, said Vera – and at three o'clock next morning, in the deepest part of the night, the two envoys of the Israelite religious community whom she had been expecting for some time arrived with the news that Agáta must prepare to be taken away within six days. These messengers, as Vera described them to me, said Austerlitz, who were strikingly alike and had faces that seemed somehow indistinct, with flickering outlines, wore jackets furnished with assorted pleats, pockets, button facings and a belt, garments which looked especially versatile although it was not clear what purpose they served. The pair spoke quietly to Agáta for some time, and gave her a sheaf of printed forms and instructions setting out everything down to the very smallest detail: where and when the person summoned must present herself, what items of clothing were to be brought – coat, raincoat, warm headgear, ear muffs, mittens, nightdress, underclothes, and so on – what articles of personal use it was advisable to bring, for instance sewing things, leather grease, a spirit stove and candles; the weight of the main item of luggage, which was not to exceed fifty kilos; what else could be brought in the way of hand baggage and provisions; how the luggage was to be labelled, with name, destination, and the number allotted to her; the proviso that all the attached forms were to be filled in and signed, that it was not permitted to bring cushions or other articles of furnishing, or to make rucksacks and travelling bags out of Persian rugs, winter coats, or other valuable remnants of fabric; and furthermore that matches, lighters and smoking were prohibited at the embarkation point and thereafter in general, and all orders issued by the official authorities were to be followed to the letter in every contingency. Agáta was unable, as I could see for myself, said Vera, to follow these nauseatingly phrased directives; instead, she simply flung a few wholly impractical items into a bag at random, like someone going away for the weekend, so that finally, difficult as it was for me and guilty as it made me feel, I did her packing while she simply stood at the window, turning away from me to look out at

GHETTOIZED. The German officials and their Czech and Jewish assistants walked busily to and fro, and there was much shouting and cursing, and blows as well. Those who were to leave had to stay in the places allotted to them. Most of them were silent, some wept quietly, but outbursts of despair, loud shouting and fits of frenzied rage were not uncommon. They stayed in this cold Trade Fair building for several days, until finally, early one morning when scarcely anyone was out and about, they were marched under guard to nearby Holešovice railway station, where it took almost another three hours to load them on the trucks. Later, said Vera, I often walked out to Holešovice, to Stromovka Park and the Trade Fair precinct. On these occasions I usually visited the lapidarium installed there in the sixties and spent hours looking at the mineral samples in the glass cases – pyrite crystals, deep green Siberian malachites, specimens of Bohemian mica, granite, quartz, and limestone of an isabelline yellow hue – wondering at the nature of the foundations on which our world is built. On the very day when Agáta had been forced to leave her flat, Vera told me, said Austerlitz, a man from the Trusteeship Centre for Requisitioned Goods came to the Šporkova and put a

Street, she handed me, after a long pause in which the silence in the Šporkova flat seemed to grow deeper with every breath we drew, two small photographs measuring about three by four inches from the little occasional table beside her chair. She had found them by chance the previous evening inside one of the fifty-five carmine-red volumes of Balzac which she had happened to pick up, she did not know why. Vera said she could not remember unfastening the glass doors and taking the book off the shelf where it stood with its companions, she merely saw herself sitting here in this armchair and – for the first time since her late twenties, a point on which she laid special emphasis – turning the pages which tell the story of the great injustice suffered by Colonel Chabert. How the two pictures had slipped between the leaves was a mystery to her, said Vera. Perhaps Agáta had borrowed the small volume while she was still living here in the Šporkova, in the last weeks before the Germans marched in. In any case, one of the photographs showed the stage of a provincial theatre, perhaps in Reichenau or Olmütz or one of the other towns where Agáta sometimes performed before she was engaged to appear in Prague. At first glance, said Austerlitz, Vera said she

had thought the two figures in the bottom left-hand corner were Agáta and Maximilian – they were so tiny that it was impossible to make them out well – but then of course she noticed that they were other people, perhaps the impresario, or a conjuror and his woman assistant. She had wondered, said Vera, what kind of play or opera had been staged in front of this alarming backdrop, and because of the high mountain range and the wild forest background she thought it might have been *Wilhelm Tell*, or *La Sonnambula*, or Ibsen's last play. The Swiss boy with the apple on his head appeared in my mind's eye, Vera continued; I sensed in me the moment of terror in which the narrow bridge gives way under the sleepwalker's foot, and imagined that, high in the rocks above, an avalanche was already breaking loose, about to sweep the poor folk who had lost their way (for what else would have brought them to these desolate surroundings?) down into the depths next moment. Minutes went by, said Austerlitz, in which I too thought I saw the cloud of snow crashing into the valley, before I heard Vera again, speaking of the mysterious quality peculiar to such photographs when they surface from oblivion. One has the impression, she said, of something stirring in them, as if one caught small sighs of despair, *gémissements de désespoir* was her expression, said Austerlitz, as if the pictures had a memory of their own and remembered us, remembered the roles that we, the survivors, and those no longer among us had played in our former lives. Yes, and the small boy in

cape over his arm which appears to be held at an angle or, as I once thought, said Austerlitz, might have been broken or in a splint, the six large mother-of-pearl buttons, the extravagant hat with the heron's feather in it, even the folds of the stockings. I examined every detail under a magnifying glass without once finding the slightest clue. And in doing so I always felt the piercing, inquiring gaze of the page boy who had come to demand his dues, who was waiting in the grey light of dawn on the empty field for me to accept the challenge and avert the misfortune lying ahead of him. That evening in the Šporkova, when Vera put the picture of the child cavalier in front of me, I was not, as you might suppose, moved or distressed, said Austerlitz, only speechless and uncomprehending, incapable of any lucid thought. Even later nothing but blind panic filled me when I thought of the five-year-old page. Once I dreamed of returning to the flat in Prague after a long absence. All the furniture is in its proper place. I know that my parents will soon be back from their holiday, and there is something important which I must give them. I am not aware that they have been dead for years. I simply think they must be very old, around ninety or a hundred, as indeed they

would be if they were still alive. But when at last
they come through the door they are in their mid-
thirties at the most. They enter the flat, walk round
the rooms picking up this and that, sit in the
drawing-room for a while and talk to each other in
the mysterious language of deaf mutes. They take no
notice of me. I suspect that they are about to set off
again for the place somewhere in the mountains
where they now live. It does not seem to me,
Austerlitz added, that we understand the laws
governing the return of the past, but I feel more and
more as if time did not exist at all, only various
spaces interlocking according to the rules of a higher
form of stereometry, between which the living
and the dead can move back and forth as they like,
and the longer I think about it the more it seems to
me that we who are still alive are unreal in the eyes
of the dead, that only occasionally, in certain lights
and atmospheric conditions, do we appear in their
field of vision. As far back as I can remember, said
Austerlitz, I have always felt as if I had no place in
reality, as if I were not there at all, and I never had
this impression more strongly than on that evening
in the Šporkova when the eyes of the Rose Queen's
page looked through me. Even next day, on my way

to Terezín, I could not imagine who or what I was. I remember that I stood in a kind of trance on the platform of the bleak station at Holešovice, that the railway lines ran away into infinity on both sides, that I perceived everything indistinctly, and then that I leaned against a window in the corridor of the train, looking out at the northern suburbs as they passed by, at the water meadows of the Vltava and the villas and summer houses on the opposite bank. Once I saw a huge and now disused stone quarry on the other side of the river, then a number of cherry trees in blossom, a few villages far remote from one another, nothing else but the empty Bohemian countryside. When I got out of the train in Lovosice after about an hour, I felt as if I had been travelling for weeks, going further and further east and further

and further back in time. The square in front of the station was empty except for a peasant woman wearing several layers of coats, and waiting behind a makeshift stall for someone to think about buying one of the cabbages she had piled up into a mighty bulwark in front of her. There was no taxi in sight, so I set off on foot from Lovosice in the direction of Terezín. As one leaves the town, the appearance of which I can no longer remember, said Austerlitz, a wide panorama opens up to the north: a field, poison-green in colour, in the foreground, behind it a petrochemicals plant half eaten away by rust, with clouds of smoke rising from its cooling towers and chimneys, as they must have done without cease for many long years. Further away I saw the conical Bohemian mountains surrounding the Bohuševice

basin in a semicircle, their highest summits disappearing into the low sky this cold, grey morning. I walked on down the straight road, always looking ahead to see if the silhouette of the fortifications, which could not be more than an hour and a half's walk away, was in sight yet. The idea I had formed in my mind was of a mighty complex rising high above the level country, but in fact Terezín lies so far down in the damp lowlands around the confluence of the Eger and the Elbe that, as I read later, there is nothing to be seen of the town, even from the hills around Leitmeritz or indeed from its immediate vicinity, except the chimney of the brewery and the church tower. The brick walls built in the eighteenth century to a star-shaped ground plan, undoubtedly by serf labour, rise from a broad moat and stand not much higher than the outlying fields. In the course of time, moreover, all kinds of shrubs and bushes have covered the former glacis and the grass-grown ramparts, giving the impression that Terezín is not so much a fortified town as one half-hidden and sunk into the marshy ground of the flood plain. At any rate, as I made my way that morning to Terezín along the main road from Lovosice, I

did not know until the last minute how close I already was to my journey's end. Several syca-mores and chestnuts, their bark blackened by

rain, still obstructed my view when I found myself standing among the façades of the old garrison buildings, and a few more steps brought me out on the central square, which was surrounded by a double avenue of trees. From the first, I felt that the most striking aspect of the place was its emptiness, said Austerlitz, something which to this day I still find incomprehensible. I knew from Vera that for many years now Terezín had been an ordinary town again. Despite this, it was almost a quarter of an hour before I saw the first human being on the other side of the square, a bent figure toiling very slowly forward and leaning on a stick, yet when I took my eye off it for a moment the figure had suddenly gone. Otherwise I met no one all morning in the straight, deserted streets of Terezín, except for a mentally disturbed man who crossed my path among the lime trees of the park with the fountain, telling I have no idea what tale in a kind of broken German while frantically waving his arms, before he too, still clutching the hundred-crown note I had given him, seemed to be swallowed up by the earth, as they say, even as he was running off. Although the sense of abandonment in this

fortified town, laid out like Campanella's ideal
sun state to a strictly geometrical grid, was extraordinarily oppressive, yet more so was the forbidding aspect of the silent façades. Not a single
curtain moved behind their blank windows,
however often I glanced up at them. I could not

imagine, said Austerlitz, who might inhabit these
desolate buildings, or if anyone lived there at
all, although on the other hand I had noticed
that long rows of dustbins with large numbers
on them in red paint were ranged against the
walls of the back yards. What I found most uncanny of all, however, were the gates and door-
ways of Terezín, all of them, as I thought I sensed,

obstructing access to a darkness never yet
penetrated, a darkness in which I thought, said

Austerlitz, there was no more movement at all apart from the whitewash peeling off the walls and the spiders spinning their threads, scuttling on crooked legs across the floorboards, or hanging expectantly in their webs. Not long ago, on the verge of waking from sleep, I found myself looking into the interior of one of these Terezín barracks. It was filled from floor to ceiling with layer upon layer of the cobwebs woven by those ingenious creatures. I still remember how, in my half-conscious state, I tried to hold fast to my powdery grey dream image, which sometimes quivered in a slight breath of air, and to discover

what it concealed, but it only dissolved all the more and was overlaid by the memory, surfacing in my mind at the same time, of the shining glass in the display windows of the ANTIKOS BAZAR on the west side of the town square, where I had stood for a long time around midday in what proved to be the vain hope that someone might arrive and open this curious emporium. As far as I could see, said Austerlitz, the ANTIKOS BAZAR is the only shop of any kind in Terezín apart from a tiny grocery store. It occupies the entire façade of one of the largest buildings, and I think its vaults reach back a long way as well. Of

course I could see nothing but the items on display in the windows, which can have amounted to only a small part of the junk heaped up inside the shop. But even these four still lifes obviously composed entirely at random, which appeared to have grown quite naturally into the black branches of the lime trees standing around the square and reflected in the glass of the windows, exerted such a power of attraction on me that it was a long time before I could tear myself away from staring at the hundreds of different objects, my forehead pressed against the cold window, as if one of them or their relationship with each other must provide an unequivocal answer to the

many questions I found it impossible to ask in my mind. What was the meaning of the festive white lace tablecloth hanging over the back of the ottoman, and the armchair with its worn brocade cover? What secret lay behind the three brass mortars of different sizes, which had about them the suggestion of an oracular utterance, or the cut-glass bowls, ceramic vases and earthenware jugs, the tin advertising sign bearing the words *Theresienstädter Wasser*, the little box of seashells, the miniature barrel organ, the globe-shaped paperweights with wonderful marine flowers swaying inside their glassy spheres, the model ship (some kind of corvette under full sail), the oak-leaf-embroidered jacket of light, pale, summery linen, the stag-horn buttons, the outsize Russian officer's cap and the olive-green uniform tunic with gilt epaulettes that went with it, the fishing rod, the hunter's bag, the Japanese fan, the endless landscape painted round a lampshade in fine brush-strokes, showing a river running quietly through perhaps Bohemia or perhaps Brazil? And then there was the stuffed squirrel, already moth-eaten here and there, perched on the stump of a branch in a showcase the size of a shoebox, which had its beady button eye implacably fixed on me, and whose Czech name – *veverka* – I now recalled like the name of a long-lost friend. What, I asked myself, said Austerlitz, might be the significance of the river never rising from any source, never flowing out into any sea but always back into itself, what was the meaning of *veverka*, the squirrel forever perched in the same position, or of the ivory-coloured porcelain group of a hero on horseback turning to look back, as his steed

rears up on its hindquarters, in order to raise up with his outstretched left arm an innocent girl already bereft of her last hope, and to save her from a cruel fate not revealed to the observer? They were all as timeless as that moment of

year and in such weather. And the people of Terezín
didn't come anyway, she added, picking up the
white handkerchief she was edging with loops like
flower petals. So I went round the exhibition by
myself, said Austerlitz, through the rooms on the
mezzanine floor and the floor above, stood in front
of the display panels, sometimes skimming over the
captions, sometimes reading them letter by letter,
stared at the photographic reproductions, could not
believe my eyes, and several times had to turn away
and look out of a window into the garden behind the
building, having for the first time acquired some idea
of the history of the persecution which my avoidance
system had kept from me for so long, and which
now, in this place, surrounded me on all sides. I
studied the maps of the Greater German Reich and
its protectorates, which had never before been more
than blank spaces in my otherwise well-developed
sense of topography, I traced the railway lines
running through them, felt blinded by the docu-
mentation recording the population policy of the
National Socialists, by the evidence of their mania
for order and purity, which was put into practice on
a vast scale through measures partly improvised,
partly devised with obsessive organizational zeal. I

was confronted with incontrovertible proof of the setting up of a forced labour system throughout Central Europe, and learned of the deliberate wastage and discarding of the work-slaves themselves, of the origins and places of death of the victims, the routes by which they were taken to what destinations, what names they had borne in life and what they and their guards looked like. I understood it all now, yet I did not understand it, for every detail that was revealed to me as I went through the museum from room to room and back again, ignorant as I feared I had been through my own fault, far exceeded my comprehension. I saw pieces of luggage brought to Terezín by the internees from Prague and Pilsen, Würzburg and Vienna, Kufstein and Karlsbad and countless other places; the items such as handbags, belt buckles, clothes brushes and combs which they had made in the various workshops; meticulously worked out projects and production plans for the agricultural exploitation of the open areas behind the ramparts and on the glacis, where oats and hemp, hops and pumpkins and maize were to be grown on plots of land meticulously parcelled out. I saw balance sheets, registers of the dead, lists of every imaginable kind, and endless rows of numbers and figures, which must have served to reassure the administrators that nothing ever escaped their notice. And whenever I think of the museum in Terezín now, said Austerlitz, I see the framed ground-plan of the star-shaped fortifications, colour-washed in soft tones of grey-brown for Maria Theresia, her Imperial Highness in Vienna who had commissioned it, and fitting neatly into the folds of the surrounding terrain, the model of a world made by reason and regulated in all conceivable respects. This impregnable fortress has never been besieged, not even by the Prussians in 1866, but throughout the nineteenth century – if one disregards the fact that a considerable number of political prisoners of the Habsburg empire pined away in the casemates of one of its outworks – remained a quiet garrison for two or three regiments and some two thousand civilians throughout the nineteenth century, somewhat out of the way, a town with yellow-painted walls, galleried courtyards, well-clipped trees, bakeries, beerhouses, casinos, soldiers' quarters, armouries, bandstand concerts, occasional forays for the purpose of military manoeuvres, officers' wives who were bored to death, and service regulations which, it was believed, would never change for all eternity. When, towards the end of the day, the museum guardian came up to me and indicated that she would soon have to close, said Austerlitz, I had just been reading, several times over, a note on one of the display panels, to the effect that in the middle of December 1942, and thus at the very time when Agáta came to Terezín, some sixty thousand people were shut up together in the ghetto, a built-up area of one square kilometre at the most, and a little later, when I was out in the deserted town square again, it suddenly seemed to me, with the greatest clarity, that they had never been taken away after all, but were still living crammed into those buildings and basements and attics, as if they were incessantly going up and down the stairs, looking out of the windows, moving in vast numbers through the streets and alleys, and even, a silent assembly, filling the entire space occupied by the air, hatched with grey as it was by the fine rain. With this picture before my eyes I boarded the old-fashioned bus which had appeared out of nowhere, and stopped by the pavement directly in front of me a few paces from the entrance to the museum. It was one of those buses which travel from the country into the

towards morning did I sleep briefly, but even then, in the deepest unconsciousness, the flow of pictures did not cease but instead condensed into a nightmare in which, from where I do not know, said Austerlitz, the north Bohemian town of Dux appeared to me situated in the middle of a devastated plain, a place of which all I had previously known was that Casanova spent the last years of his life there in Count Waldstein's castle writing his memoirs, a number of mathematical and esoteric tracts, and his five-volume futuristic novel *Icosameron*. In my dream I saw the old roué shrunk to the size of a boy, surrounded by the gold-stamped rows of books in Count Waldstein's library of more than forty thousand volumes, bending over his writing desk alone on a bleak November afternoon. He had taken off his powdered wig, and his own sparse hair was wafting above his head in a little white cloud, like a sign of the dissolution of his corporeal being. He wrote on and on, his left shoulder slightly raised. There was nothing to be heard but the scratching of his pen, which stopped only when the writer looked up for a couple of seconds and his watery eyes, already half blind for long-distance vision, sought what little brightness was still left in the sky above the park of

Dux. On the other side of the enclosed land, in deep darkness, lay the whole region extending from Teplice to Most and Chomutov. Over to the north, from end to end of the horizon, stood the black wall of the Grenzmark mountains, and in front of them, along their foothills, the torn and ravaged land, with slopes and terraces which dropped far below what had formerly been the surface of the earth. Where roads had once passed over firm ground, where human beings had lived, foxes had run across country and birds of many kinds had flown from bush to bush, now there was nothing but empty space, and at the bottom of it stones and gravel and stagnant water, untouched even by the natural movement of the air. The shadowy forms of power stations with their glowing furnaces drifted like ships in the sombre air: chalk-coloured buildings like blocks, cooling towers with jagged rims, tall chimneys above which motionless plumes of smoke stood white against the sickly colours streaking the western sky. A few stars showed only on the pallid, nocturnal side of the firmament, sooty, smoking lights extinguished one by one, leaving scab-like traces in the orbits through which they have always moved. To the south, in a broad semicircle, rose the cones of the extinct Bohemian volcanoes, which I wished in my nightmare would erupt and cover everything around with black dust. — Not until around half-past two next day, when I had to some degree pulled myself together again, did I go from Kampa Island to the Šporkova to pay what would be my last visit there for the time being, Austerlitz continued. I had already told Vera that I must retrace my journey from Prague to London by train, all the way across Germany, a country unknown to me, but that then I would soon come back and perhaps take a flat somewhere near her for a few months. It was one of those radiant spring days when the weather is clear as glass. Vera was complaining of a dull pain behind her eyes which had been troubling her since early that morning, and she asked me to pull the curtains over the windows on the sunny side of the room. Leaning back in her red velvet armchair in the gloom, with her tired eyelids closed, she listened as I told her what I had seen in Terezín. I also asked Vera about the Czech word for a squirrel, and after a while, with a smile spreading slowly over her beautiful face, she said it was *veverka*. And then, said Austerlitz, Vera told me how in autumn we would often stand by the upper enclosure wall of the Schönborn Garden to incapable of thinking of Agáta, of what must have become of her, and of her own life continuing into a pointless future. For weeks she was hardly in her right mind, she had felt a kind of dragging outside her body, she had tried to pick up broken threads and could not believe that everything had really happened as it did. None of her endless attempts later to find out my whereabouts in England or my father's in France had produced any results. Whatever she tried, it was as if all traces were lost in the sand, for at the time, with an army of censors causing havoc in the postal services, it often took months to get an answer from abroad. Perhaps, Vera surmised, said Austerlitz, it would have been different if she could have turned in person to the appropriate authorities, but she lacked both the opportunity and the means to do so. And in this way the years had raced by, seeming in retrospect like a single leaden day. She had indeed gone into the teaching profession and did what was necessary to maintain herself, but almost all her feelings had been extinguished, and she had not truly breathed since that time. Only in the books written in earlier times did she sometimes think she found some faint idea of what it might be like to be alive. Such remarks of Vera's were often followed by a long silence, said Austerlitz, as if neither of us knew what to say, and the hours passed by almost imperceptibly in the darkened flat in the Šporkova. Towards evening, when I said goodbye to Vera, holding her weightless hands in mine, she suddenly remembered how, on the day of my departure from the Wilsonova station, Agáta had turned to her when the train had disappeared from view, and said: We left from here for Marienbad only last summer. And now – where will we be going now? This reminiscence, which I did not fully take in at first, was soon occupying my mind so much that I made a call to Vera from the hotel on the island that evening, although in the normal way I never use the telephone. Yes, she said, in a voice very faint with weariness, yes, in the summer of 1938 we all went to Marienbad together, Agáta, Maximilian, Vera herself and me. We had spent three wonderful, almost blissful weeks there. The overweight or underweight spa guests, moving at a curiously slow pace through the grounds with their drinking glasses, radiated an extraordinary peacefulness, as Agáta once remarked in passing. We stayed at the Osborne-Balmoral boarding house behind the Palace Hotel. In the morning we generally went to the baths, and we took long walks in the country around Marienbad in the afternoons. I had retained no memory at all of that summer holiday when I was just four years old, said Austerlitz, and perhaps that was why when I was in that very place later, in Marienbad at the end of August 1972, I felt nothing but blind terror in the face of the better turn my life should have taken at that time. Marie de Verneuil, with whom I had been in correspondence since the time I spent in Paris, had invited me to accompany her on a visit to Bohemia, where she had to carry out some research for her studies on the architectural history of the spas of Europe, and I think I may now say, added Austerlitz, that she also hoped to try to liberate me from my self-inflicted isolation. She had arranged everything to perfection. Her cousin Frédéric Félix, attaché to the French embassy in Prague, had sent an enormous Tatra limousine to meet us at the airport and take us straight to Marienbad. We sat in the deeply upholstered back of the car for two or three hours as it drove west through the empty countryside, on a road which ran perfectly straight for long stretches of our journey, sometimes dipping down into valleys, then climbing again to extended plateaux over which one could

wooded slopes, darkness had fallen, and I remember, said Austerlitz, that a slight sense of disquiet
brushed me as we emerged from the firs growing all
the way down to the outlying houses and slid into the
town, which was sparsely illuminated by a few street
lamps. The car stopped outside the Palace Hotel.
Marie exchanged a few words with the chauffeur as
he took out our luggage, and then we were in the
foyer, which was made to look double its size, so to
speak, by a row of tall mirrors along the walls. The
place was so deathly still and deserted that you might
have thought the time long after midnight. It was
some while before the reception clerk at his desk in
a cramped booth looked up from what he was reading and turned to his late-come guests with a barely
audible murmur of *Dobrý vecer*. This remarkably thin
man – the first thing you noticed about him was that
although he could not have been much over forty his
forehead was wrinkled in fan-like folds above the
root of his nose – went through the necessary for-
malities without another word, very slowly, almost
as if he were moving in a denser atmosphere than
ours, asked to see our visas, looked at our passports
and his register, made an entry of some length on the
squared paper of a school exercise book in laborious

handwriting, gave us a questionnaire to fill in, looked in a drawer for our key and finally, ringing a bell, summoned as it seemed from nowhere a porter with a bent back, who was wearing a mouse-grey nylon coat that came down to his knees and, like the clerk at the reception desk, appeared to be afflicted by a chronic lethargy which incapacitated his limbs. When he preceded us up to the third floor with our two lightweight suitcases – the paternoster lift, Marie had pointed out to me as soon as we entered the foyer, had obviously been out of order for a very long time – he found it increasingly hard to climb the stairs and, like a mountaineer negotiating the last difficult ridge before attaining the summit, he had to stop several times for a rest, whereupon we too waited for a while a couple of steps below him. On the way up we met not a living soul except for another member of the hotel staff who, dressed in the same grey coat as his colleague and perhaps worn, I thought to myself, said Austerlitz, by all the employees of the state-owned spa hotels, was sitting asleep in a chair on the top landing with his head sunk forward, and a tin tray of broken glass on the floor beside him. The room unlocked for us was Number Thirty-Eight – a large room resembling a salon. The and the urinary system, glandular swellings and scrofulous deformities, not to mention weakness of the nervous and muscular systems, fatigue, trembling of the limbs, paralysis, mucous and bloody fluxes, unsightly eruptions on the skin, and practically every other medical disorder known to the human race. I can just see them in my mind's eye, said Marie, a set of very corpulent men disregarding their doctors' advice and giving themselves up to the pleasures of the table, which even at a spa were lavish at the time, in order to suppress, by dint of their increasing girth, the anxiety for the security of their social position constantly stirring within them, and I see other patients, most of them ladies and rather pale and sallow already, deep in their own thoughts as they walk along the winding paths from one of the little temples which house fountains to the next, or else in elegiac mood, watching the play of the clouds moving over the narrow valley from the viewing points of the Amalienhöhe or Schloss Miramont. The rare sense of happiness that I felt as I listened to my companion talking, said Austerlitz, paradoxically enough gave me the idea that I myself, like the guests staying in Marienbad a hundred years ago, had contracted an insidious illness, and together postage stamps, in tiny print which I could decipher only with great difficulty. The announcements were not just in French but also in German, Polish and Dutch. I still remember, said Austerlitz, Frederieke van Wincklmann, whose death notice said that she had *kalm en rustig van ons heengegaan*, I remember the strange word *rouwkamer* and the information that *De bloemen worden na de crematieplechtigheid neergelegd aan de voet van het Indisch Monument te Den Haag*. I had gone over to the window, where I looked down the main street, still wet with rain, and saw the grand hotels ranged in a semi-circle rising to the heights, the Pacifik, the Atlantic, the Metropole, the Polonia and Bohemia with their rows of balconies, their corner turrets and roof ridges emerging from the morning mist like ocean-going steamers from a dark sea. At some time in the past, I thought, I must have made a mistake, and now I am living the wrong life. Later, on a walk through the deserted town and up to the fountain colonnade, I kept feeling as if someone else were walking beside me, or as if something had brushed against me. Every new view that opened out before us as we turned a corner, every façade, every flight of steps looked to me both familiar and utterly alien. I felt that the decrepit state of these once magnificent buildings, with their broken gutters, walls blackened by rainwater, crumbling plaster revealing the coarse masonry beneath it, windows boarded up or clad with corrugated iron, precisely reflected my own state of mind, which I could not explain either to myself or to Marie, not on this first walk we took through the deserted park nor in the late afternoon, when we sat in the dimly lit *kavárna* of the Město Moskva under a picture of pink water-lilies measuring at least four square yards. I remember, said Austerlitz, that we ordered an ice cream, or rather, as it turned out, a confection resembling an ice cream, a plaster-like substance tasting of potato starch and notable chiefly for the fact that even after more than an hour it did not melt. Apart from us the only customers in the Město Moskva were two old gentlemen playing chess at one of the tables at the back. The waiter who was standing by the net curtains, which were discoloured with smoke, his hands behind his back and looking out, lost in thought, at the rubbish dump overgrown with giant hogweed on the other side of the road, was himself advanced in age. His white hair and moustache were carefully trimmed, and although he too wore one of those mouse-grey nylon coats it was may have dated from the Metternich period, was in an advanced state of decay. The floor inside the brick walls was covered with pigeon droppings compressed under their own weight, yet already over two feet high, a hard, desiccated mass on which lay the bodies of some of the birds who had fallen from their niches, mortally sick, while their companions, surviving in a kind of senile dementia, cooed at one another in tones of quiet complaint in the darkness under the roof, and a few downy feathers, spinning round in a little whirlwind, slowly sank through the air. The torment inherent in both these images that came into my mind in Marienbad, the mad Schumann and the pigeons immured in that place of horror, made it impossible for me to attain even the lowest step on the way to self-knowledge. On the final day of our visit, Austerlitz continued at last, in the evening and as if to say goodbye, we walked through the park and down to the Auschowitz Springs. There is a prettily built and fully glazed pump-room there, all painted white inside. In this pump-room, illuminated by the rays of the setting sun, where, apart from the regular splashing of the water, silence reigned entirely, Marie moved closer to me and asked whether I had remembered that

tomorrow was my birthday. When we wake up
tomorrow, she said, I shall wish you every happiness, and it will be like telling a machine working
by some unknown mechanism that I hope it will
run well. Can't you tell me the reason, she asked,
said Austerlitz, why you remain so unapproach-
able? Why, she said, have you been like a pool of
frozen water ever since we came here? Why do I
see your lips opening as if you were about to say
something, maybe even cry out loud, and then I hear
not the slightest sound? Why did you never unpack
when we arrived, always preferring to live out of a
rucksack, as it were? We stood there a couple of
paces apart, like two actors on stage. The colour of

ahead of us, and Marie, whom I lost entirely soon afterwards, by my own fault, was murmuring something quietly to herself. All I remember of it now is a phrase about the poor lovers *qui se promenaient dans les allées désertes du parc*. We were almost back in the town, said Austerlitz, when a little company of some ten or a dozen small people emerged from the dark as if out of nowhere, at a place where white mist was already rising from the ground, and crossed our path. They were the sort of visitors sent to the spa because of their failing health by some Czech enterprise or other, or perhaps they came from one of the neighbouring Socialist countries. They were strikingly short, almost dwarfish figures, slightly bent, moving along in single file, and each of them held one of those pitiful plastic mugs from which the water of the springs was drunk in Mariánske Lázne at the time. I also remember, added Austerlitz, that without exception they wore raincoats of thin bluegrey Perlon, the kind of thing that had been fashionable in the West in the late 1950s. To this day I can sometimes hear the dry rustling with which, as suddenly as they had appeared on one side of the path, they vanished again on the other. — I dwelt on my memories of Marienbad all night after my last visit to the Šporkova, continued Austerlitz. As soon as it began to grow light outside I packed, left the hotel on Kampa Island, and crossed the Charles Bridge, which was wrapped in early mist, walked through the streets of the Old Town and over the still deserted Wenceslaus Square, making my way to the main station on Wilsonova which, as it turned out, did not correspond in the least to the idea I had formed of it from Vera's narrative. Its Jugendstil architecture, once famous far beyond Prague, had been surrounded, obviously in the 1960s, by ugly glass façades and concrete blocks, and it took me some time to find a way into this forbidding complex over a taxi ramp leading down to the basement storey. The low-ceilinged hall I now entered was crowded with throngs of people who had spent the night there among piles of luggage, huddled together in groups of various sizes, most of them still asleep. A sickening red-hued light immersed the entire apparently boundless encampment in a positively infernal glare as it shone from a slightly raised plat-form measuring at least ten by twenty metres, on which about a hundred games machines were arranged in several batteries, idling to no purpose and chanting inanely to themselves. I stepped over had been like when, carried in Agáta's arms – as Vera had told me, said Austerlitz – I craned my neck, unable to take my eyes off the vault reaching such a vast height above us. But neither Agáta nor Vera nor I myself emerged from the past. Sometimes it seemed as if the veil would part; I thought, for one fleeting instant, that I could feel the touch of Agáta's shoulder or see the picture on the front of the Charlie Chaplin comic which Vera had bought me for the journey, but as soon as I tried to hold one of these fragments fast, or get it into better focus, as it were, it disappeared into the emptiness revolving over my head. It was all the more surprising and indeed alarming a little later, said Austerlitz, when I looked out of the corridor window of my carriage just before the train left at seven-thirteen, to find it dawning upon me with perfect certainty that I had seen the pattern of the glass and steel roof above the platforms before, made up as it was of tri-angles, round arches, horizontal and vertical lines and diagonals, and in the same half-light. As the train rolled very slowly out of the station, through a passage between the backs of blocks of flats and into the dark tunnel running under the New Town, and then crossed the Vltava with a regular beat, it really

seemed to me, said Austerlitz, as if time had stood still since the day when I first left Prague. It was a dark, oppressive morning. A small lamp with a pink pleated shade, the kind of thing one used to see in the windows of Belgian brothels, stood on the white cloth covering the little table in the Czech State Railways dining car, where I was sitting in order to get a better view. The chef, his toque at an angle on his head, leaned in the entrance to his galley smoking and talking to the waiter, a curly-haired, slight little man in a check waistcoat and yellow bow-tie. Outside, under the lowering sky, meadows and fields passed by, fishponds, woods, the curve of a bend in a river, a stand of alders, hills and valleys, and at Beroun, if I remember correctly, a lime-works extending over a square mile or more, with chimneys and towering silos disappearing into the low clouds above, huge square buildings of crumbling concrete roofed with rusty corrugated iron, conveyor belts moving up and down, mills to grind the stone, conical mounds of gravel, huts and freight trucks, all of it uniformly covered with pale-grey sinter and dust. Then the wide countryside opened out again, and all the time I was looking out I never saw a vehicle on the roads, or a single human being except for the station masters who, whether from boredom or habit or because of some regulation which they had to observe, had come out on the platform at even the smallest stations such as Holoubkov, Chrást or Rokycany in their red uniform caps, most of them, it seemed to me, sporting blond moustaches, and determined not to miss the Prague express as it thundered by on this pallid April morning. All I remember of Pilsen, where we stopped for some time, said Austerlitz, is that I went out on the platform to photograph the capital of a cast-iron column which had touched some chord of recognition in me. What made me uneasy at the sight of it, however, was not the question of whether the complex form of the capital, now covered with a puce-tinged encrustation, had really impressed itself on my mind when I passed through Pilsen with the children's transport in the summer of 1939, but the idea, ridiculous in itself, that this cast-iron column, which with its scaly surface seemed almost to approach the nature of a living being, might remember me and was, if I may so put it, said Austerlitz, a witness to what I could no longer recollect for myself. Beyond Pilsen the reached Nuremberg, and when I saw the name on a signal box in its German spelling of Nürnberg, which was unfamiliar to me, I remembered what Vera had said about my father's account of the National Socialist Party rally of 1936 and the roars of acclamation rising from the people who had gathered here at the time. Although I had really meant to do no more than ask about my next connections, said Austerlitz, that recollection may have been why I walked out of Nuremberg station without pausing to think and on into that unknown city. I had never before set foot on German soil, I had always avoided learning anything at all about German topography, German history or modern German life, and so, said Austerlitz, Germany was probably more unfamiliar to me than any other country in the world, more foreign even than Afghanistan or Paraguay. As soon as I had emerged from the underpass in front of the station I was swept along by a huge crowd of people who were streaming down the entire breadth of the street, rather like water in a river bed, going in not just one but both directions, as if flowing simultaneously up- and downstream. I think it was a Saturday, the day when people go to shop in town, inundating these pedestrian zones which apparently, as I was told later, said Austerlitz, exist in more or less the same form in all German cities. The first thing that caught my eye on this excursion was the great number of grey, brown and green loden coats and hats, and how well and sensibly everyone was dressed in general, how remarkably solid were the shoes of the pedestrians of Nuremberg. I avoided looking closely at the faces coming towards me, and thought it odd that few of these people raised their voices as they moved quietly through the city. Looking up at the façades on both sides of the street, even those of the older buildings which, judging by their style, must date from the sixteenth or fifteenth century, I was troubled to realize that I could not see a crooked line anywhere, not at the corners of the houses or on the gables, the window frames or the sills, nor was there any other trace of past history. I remember, said Austerlitz, that the paving under my feet sloped slightly downhill, that once, looking over the parapet of a bridge, I caught sight of two snow-white swans swimming on black water, and then, high above the rooftops, of the castle, somehow miniaturized and in postage-stamp format, so to speak. I could not bring myself to go into a café or buy anything from one of the many stalls and booths. When I turned to go back to the station after about an hour, I felt increasingly as if I had to struggle against a current growing ever stronger, perhaps because I was now going uphill, or maybe there were in fact more people moving one way than the other. In any case, said Austerlitz, I felt more panic-stricken with every passing minute, so that at last, although I was not at all far from the station, I had to stop under the red sandstone arch of a window displaying the pages of the local Nuremberg newspaper, where I waited until the crowds of shoppers had to some extent thinned out. I cannot now say for certain how long I stood there, my senses dazed, on the outer edge of this flood of Germans moving endlessly past me, said Austerlitz, but I think it was four or five o'clock by the time an elderly woman wearing a kind of Tyrolean hat with a cockerel's feather in it stopped beside me, probably taking me for one of the homeless because of my old rucksack, fetched a one-mark coin out of her purse with arthritic fingers, and carefully handed it to me as alms. I was still holding this coin, minted in 1956 with the of the journey he had died of consumption and was stowed in the baggage net with the rest of our belongings. And then, Austerlitz continued, somewhere beyond Frankfurt, when I entered the Rhine valley for the second time in my life, the sight of the Mäuseturm in the part of the river known as the Binger Loch revealed, with absolute

certainty, why the tower in Lake Vyrnwy had always seemed to me so uncanny. I could not take my eyes off the great river Rhine flowing sluggishly along in the dusk, the apparently motionless barges lying low in the water, which almost lapped over their decks, the trees and bushes on the other bank, the fine cross-hatching of the vineyards, the stronger transverse lines of the walls supporting the terraces, the slate-grey rocks and ravines leading off sideways into what seemed to me a pre-historic and unexplored realm. While I was still under the spell of this landscape, to me a truly mythological one, said Austerlitz, the setting sun broke through the clouds, filled the entire valley with its radiance, and illuminated the heights on the other side where three gigantic chimneys towered into the sky at the place we were just pass-ing, making the steep slopes on the eastern moun-tains look like hollow shells, mere camouflage for an underground industrial site covering many square miles. Passing through the valley of the Rhine, said Austerlitz, you can scarcely tell what century it is. As you look out of the train window it is difficult to say even of the castles standing high above the river, bearing such strange and somehow preposterous names as Reichenstein, Ehrenfels and Stahleck, whether they are medieval or were built by the industrial barons of the nineteenth century. Some of them, for instance Burg Katz and Burg Maus, seem to be rooted in legend, and even the ruins resemble a romantic stage set. At least, I no longer knew in what period of my life I was living as I journeyed down the Rhine valley. Through the evening sunlight I saw the glow of a fiery dawn rising from my past above the other bank, pervading the whole sky. Even today, Austerlitz continued, when I think of my Rhine journeys, the second of them hardly less terrifying than the first, everything becomes confused in my head: my experiences of that time, what I have read, memories surfacing and then sinking out of sight again, consecutive images and distressing blank spots where nothing at all is left. I see that German landscape, said Austerlitz, as it was described by earlier travellers, the great river not yet regulated in any way, flooding its banks in places, salmon leaping in the water, crayfish crawling over the fine sand; I see Victor Hugo's sombre pen-and-ink drawings of the Rhine castles, and Joseph Mallord Turner sitting on a folding stool not far from the murderous town of Bacharach, swiftly painting his watercolours; I see the deep waters of Lake Vyrnwy and the people of Llanwyddyn submerged in them; and I see, said Austerlitz, the great army of mice, a grey horde said to have plagued the German countryside, plunging into the river and swimming desperately, their little throats raised only just above the water, to reach the safety of the island.

— Imperceptibly, the day had begun drawing to a close as Austerlitz talked, and the light was already fading when we left the house in Alderney Street together to walk a little way out of town, along the Mile End Road to the large Tower Hamlets cemetery, which is surrounded by a tall, dark brick wall and, like the adjoining complex of St Clement's Hospital, according to a remark made by Austerlitz in passing, was one of the scenes of this phase of his story. In the twilight slowly falling over London we walked along the paths of the cemetery, past monuments

erected by the Victorians to commemorate their dead, past mausoleums, marble crosses, stelae and obelisks, bulbous urns and statues of angels, many of them wingless or otherwise mutilated, turned to stone, so it seemed to me, at the very moment when they were about to take off

"UNTIL THE DAY BREAK, AND THE SHADOWS FLEE AWAY."

from the earth. Most of these memorials had long ago been tilted to one side or thrown over entirely by the roots of the sycamores which were shooting up everywhere. The sarcophagi covered with pale-green, grey, ochre and orange lichens were broken, some of the graves themselves had risen above the ground or sunk into it, so that you might think an earthquake had shaken this abode of the departed, or else that, summoned to the Last Judgment, they had upset, as they rose from their resting places, the neat and tidy order we impose on them. In the first few weeks after his return from Bohemia, Austerlitz continued his tale as we walked on, he had learnt by heart the names and dates of birth and death of those buried here, he had taken home pebbles and ivy leaves and on one occasion a stone rose, and the stone hand broken off one of the angels, but however much my walks in Tower Hamlets might soothe me during the day, said Austerlitz, at night I was plagued by the most frightful anxiety attacks which sometimes lasted for hours on end. It was obviously of little use that I had discovered the sources of my distress and, looking back over all the past years, could now see myself with the utmost clarity as that child suddenly cast out of his familiar surroundings: reason was powerless against the sense of rejection and annihilation which I had always suppressed, and which was now breaking through the walls of its confinement. Soon I would be overcome by this terrible anxiety in the midst of the simplest actions: tying my shoelaces, washing up teacups, waiting for the kettle to boil. All of a sudden my tongue and palate would be as dry as if I had been lying in the desert for days, I had to fight harder and harder for breath, my heart began to flutter and palpitate in my throat, cold sweat broke out all over my body, even on the back of my trembling hand, and everything I looked at was veiled by a black mist. I felt like screaming but could not utter a sound, I wanted to walk out into the street but was unable to move from the spot; once, after a long and painful contraction, I actually visualized myself being broken up from within, so that parts of my body were scattered over a dark and distant terrain. I cannot say now, said Auster-litz, how many such attacks I suffered at the time, but one day, when I collapsed on my way to the kiosk at the end of Alderney Street, striking my head against the edge of the pavement, I was taken to St Clement's as the last in a series of various casu-alty departments and hospitals, and there found myself in one of the men's wards when at last I returned to my senses, after what I was told later had been nearly three weeks of mental absence which, though it did not impair the bodily func-tions, paralysed all thought processes and emotions.

I walked around in this place, said Austerlitz, his left hand pointing to the tall brick façade of the hospital building towering behind the wall, in the curiously remote state of mind induced by the drugs I was being given; both desolate and weirdly contented I wandered, all through that winter, up and down the long corridors, staring out for hours through one of the dirty windows at the cemetery below, where

we are standing now, feeling nothing inside my head but the four burnt-out walls of my brain. Later, when there had been some improvement in my condition, I looked through a telescope given to me by one of the nurses and watched the foxes running wild in the cemetery in the grey dawn. I would see squirrels dodging back and forth, or sitting quite still, arrested, as it were, in mid-motion. I studied the faces of those solitary people who visited the graveyard now and then, or I observed the slow wingbeats of an owl in its curving flight over the tombstones at nightfall. Occasionally I talked to one of the other hospital patients, a roofer, for instance, who said he could recollect with perfect clarity the moment when, just as he was about to fix a slate in place, something that had been stretched too taut inside him snapped at a particular spot behind his forehead, and for the first time he heard, coming over the crackling transistor wedged into the batten in front of him, the voices of those bearers of bad tidings which had haunted him ever since. While I was there I also thought quite often of Elias the minister lapsing into madness, and of the stone-built asylum in Denbigh where he died. But I found it impossible to think of myself, my own history, or my present state of mind. I was not discharged until the beginning of April, a year after returning from Prague. The last doctor whom I saw at the hospital advised me to look for some kind of light physical occupation, perhaps in horticulture, she suggested, and so for the next two years, at the time of day when office staff are pouring into the City, I went out the other way to Romford and my new place of work, a council-run nursery garden on the outskirts of a large park which employed, as well as the trained gardeners, a certain number of assistants who suffered from disabilities or required to have their minds set at rest by some quiet pursuit. I cannot say, said Austerlitz, why I began to recover in some degree out at Romford in the course of those months, whether it was because of the people in whose company I found myself, who though they all bore the scars of their mental sufferings often seemed carefree and very cheerful, or the constant warm, humid atmosphere in the greenhouses, the mossy, forest-ground fragrance filling the air, the rectilinear patterns presented to the eye, or simply the even tenor of the work itself, the careful prick-

ing out and potting up of seedlings, transplanting them when they had grown larger, looking after the cold frames and watering the trays with a fine hose, which I liked perhaps best of all. At the time when I

was working as an assistant gardener in Romford, said Austerlitz, I began to spend my evenings and weekends poring over the heavy tome, running to almost eight hundred close-printed pages, which H. G. Adler, a name previously unknown to me, had written between 1945 and 1947 in the most difficult of circumstances, partly in Prague and partly in London, on the subject of the setting up, development and internal organization of the Theresienstadt ghetto, and which he had revised several times before it was brought out by a German publishing house in 1955. Reading this book, which

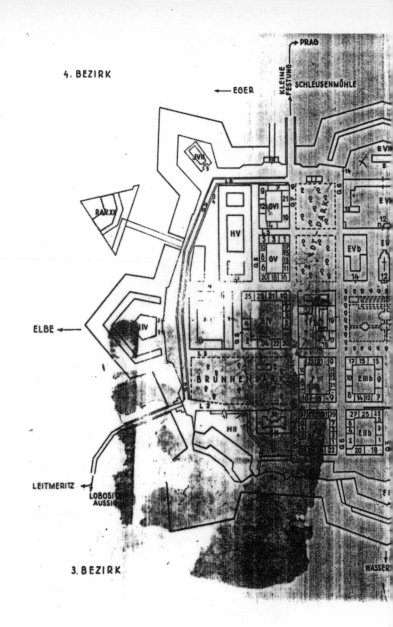

4. BEZIRK

← EGER

→ PRAG

KLEINE FESTUNG

SCHLEUSENMÜHLE

RAV.XX

ELBE ←

LEITMERITZ ←
LOBOSIT
AUSSIG

3. BEZIRK

WASSER

BRUNNENPARK

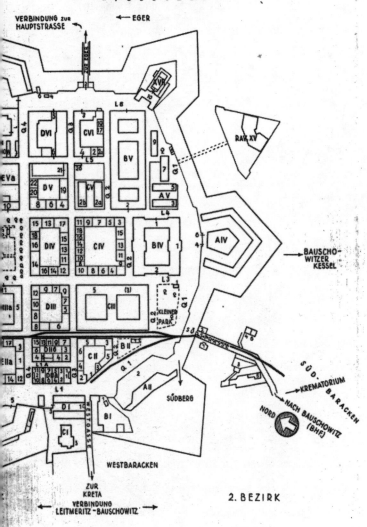

VERBINDUNG zur
HAUPTSTRASSE

← EGER

AVR

DVI   CVI

EVa   Le

BV

DV   CV

RAV. XV

AV

DIV   CIV   BIV   AIV

BAUSCHO-
WITZER
KESSEL

DIII   CIII

KLEINER
PARK

IIIa   DII   BII

IIa   CII

SÜD-
BARACKEN

AII   SÜDBERG

KREMATORIUM

L1   DI   BI

WESTSTRASSE

NORD   NACH BAUSCHOWITZ
(Bhf.)

CI

WESTBARACKEN

ZUR
KRETA
VERBINDUNG
← LEITMERITZ - BAUSCHOWITZ →

2. BEZIRK

line by line gave me an insight into matters I could never have imagined when I myself visited the fortified town, almost entirely ignorant as I was at that time, was a painstaking business because of my poor knowledge of German, and indeed, said Austerlitz, I might well say it was almost as difficult for me as deciphering an Egyptian or Babylonian text in hieroglyphic or cuneiform script. The long compounds, not listed in my dictionary, which were obviously being spawned the whole time by the pseudo-technical jargon governing everything in Theresienstadt had to be unravelled syllable by syllable. When I had finally discovered the meaning of such terms and concepts as *Barackenbestandteillager*, *Zusatzkostenberechnungsschein*, *Bagatellreparaturwerkstätte*, *Menagetransportkolonnen*, *Küchenbeschwerdeorgane*, *Reinlichkeitsreihenuntersuchung*, and *Entwesungsübersiedlung* – to my surprise, Austerlitz articulated these heterogeneous German compounds unhesitatingly and without the slightest trace of an accent – when I had worked out what they meant, he continued, I had to make just as much of an effort to fit the presumptive sense of my reconstructions into the sentences and the wider context, which kept threatening to elude me, first because it quite often took me until midnight to master a single page, and a good deal was lost in this lengthy process, and second because in its almost futuristic deformation of social life the ghetto system had something incomprehensible and unreal about it, even though Adler describes it down to the last detail in its objective actuality. It seems unpardonable to me today that I had blocked off the investigation of my most distant past for so many years, not on principle, to be sure, but still of my own accord, and that now it is too late for me to seek out Adler, who had lived in London until his death in the summer of 1988, and talk to him about that extra-territorial place where at the time, as I think I have mentioned before, said Austerlitz, some sixty thousand people were crammed together in an area little more than a square kilometre in size – industrialists and manufacturers, lawyers and doctors, rabbis and university professors, singers and composers, bank managers, businessmen, shorthand typists, housewives, farmers, labourers and millionaires, people from Prague and the rest of the Protectorate, from Slovakia, from Denmark and Holland, from Vienna and Munich, Cologne and Berlin, from the Palatinate, from Lower Franconia and Westphalia – each of

Verzeichnis der als Sonderweisungen bezeichneten Arbeiten.

1. Dienststelle
2. Kameradschaftsheim
3. SS-Garage
4. Kleine Festung
5. Deutsche Dienstpost
6. Reserve-Lazarett
7. Berliner Dienststelle
8. Gendarmerie
9. Reichssippenforschung
10. Landwirtschaft
11. Torfabladen
12. Schleusenmühle
13. Eisenbahnbau Ing. Figlovský
14. Eisenbahnbau eig. Rechnung
15. Feuerlöschteiche E I, H IV
16. Straßenbau Leitmeritz
17. Straßenbau f. Rechnung Ing. Figlovský (T 321)
18. Uhrenreparaturenwerkstätte
19. Zentralamt f. d. Regelung der Judenfrage in Prag
20. Bau des Wasserwerks (T 423)
    a) Ing. Figlovský   b) Artesia, Prag
    c) Ing. C. Pktross, Prag   d) sonstige Posten
21. Silagenbau Ing. Figlovský
    (Hilfsdienst   )
22. Kanalisationsarbeiten (T 45)
23. Kanalisationsarbeiten für Rechnung Ing. Figlovský
24. Bau der Silagegrube Ing. Figlovský
25. Steinbruch Kamaik
26. Krematoriumbau
27. Hilfsarbeiten und Schießstätte Kamaik-Leitmeritz
28. Kreta-Bauten und deren Erhaltungskosten
29. Chemische Kontrollarbeiten
30. Gruppe Dr. Weidmann [s. 19. Kap.]
31. Budterfassungsgruppe [s. 19. Kap.]
32. Schutzbrillenerzeugung
33. Uniformkonfektion
34. Rindsledergaloschen
35. Zentralbad (arische Abt.)
36. Glimmerspalten
37. Kaninchenhaarscheren
38. Tintenpulversäckchenfüllen
39. Elektrizitätswerk
40. Kartonagenwerkstätte
41. Lehrspiele
42. Marketendenwarenerzeugung (früher Galanterie)
43. Instandhaltung von Uniformen
44. Jutesäcke-Reparatur
45. Bijouterie
46. Straßenerhaltung und Straßenreinigung
47. Arbeitsgruppe Jungfern-Breschan
48. Projektierte Hydrozentrale
49. NSFK-Flugplatz
50. Schlachthof
51. Schieß-Stand
52. Holzkohleerzeugung

whom had to make do with about two square metres
of space in which to exist and all of them, in so far as
they were in any condition to do so or until they
were loaded into trucks and sent on east, obliged to

work entirely without remuneration in one of the primitive factories set up, with a view to generating actual profit, by the External Trade Section, assigned to the bandage-weaving workshop, to the handbag and satchel assembly line, the production of horn buttons and other haberdashery items, the manufacturing of wooden soles for footwear and of cowhide galoshes, to the charcoal yard, the making of such board games as Nine Men's Morris and Catch the Hat, the splitting of mica, the shearing of rabbit fur, the bottling of ink dust, the silkworm-breeding station run under the aegis of the SS or, alternatively, employed in one of the operations serving the ghetto's internal economy, in the clothing store, for instance, in one of the precinct mending and darning rooms, the shredding section, the rag depot, the book reception and sorting unit, the kitchen brigade, the potato-peeling platoon, the bone-crushing mill, the glue-boiling plant or the mattress department, as medical and nursing auxiliaries, in the disinfestation and rodent-control service, the floor-space-allocation office, the central registration bureau, the self-administration housed in barrack block BV, known as 'The Castle', or in the transport of goods maintained within the walls of the fortress by means seventy, and these people, who before they were sent away had been led to believe some tale about a pleasant resort in Bohemia called Theresienbad, with beautiful gardens, promenades, boarding houses and villas, and many of whom had been persuaded or forced to sign contracts, so-called *Heimeinkaufsverträge*, said Austerlitz, offering them, against deposits of up to eighty thousand Reichs-marks, the right of residence in what was described

to them as a most salubrious place, these people, Austerlitz continued, had come to Theresienstadt, completely misled by the illusions implanted in their minds, carrying in their luggage all manner of personal items and mementoes which could be of no conceivable use in the life that awaited them in the ghetto, often arriving already ravaged in body and spirit, no longer in their right minds, delirious, frequently unable to remember their own names, surviving the procedure of being sluiced in, as it was termed, either not at all or only by a few days, in which latter case, on account of the extreme psychopathic personality changes which they had undergone and which generally resulted in a kind of infantilism divorcing them from reality and entailing an almost total loss of the ability to speak and act, they were immediately sectioned in the casemate of the Cavalier Barracks, which served as a psychiatric ward and where they usually perished within a week under the dreadful conditions prevailing there, so that although there was no shortage of doctors and surgeons in Theresienstadt who cared for their fellow prisoners as best they could, and in spite of the steam-disinfection boiler installed in the malting kiln of the former brewery, the hydrogen-cyanide chamber and other hygienic measures introduced by the Kommandantur in an all-out campaign against infestation with lice, the number of the dead — entirely in line, said Austerlitz, with the intentions of the masters of the ghetto — rose to well above twenty thousand in the ten months between August 1942 and May 1943 alone, as a result of which the joiner's workshop in the former riding school could no longer make enough deal coffins, there were sometimes more than five hundred dead bodies stacked in layers on top of each other in the central morgue in the casemate by the gateway to the Bohusevice road, and the four naphtha-fired incinerators of the crematorium, kept going day and night in cycles of forty minutes at a time, were stretched to the utmost limits of their capacity, said Austerlitz, and this comprehensive system of internment and forced labour which, in Theresienstadt as elsewhere, was ultimately directed, so he continued, solely at the extinction of life and was built on an organizational plan regulating all functions and responsibilities, as Adler's reconstruction shows, with a crazed administrative zeal – from the use of whole troops of workers in building the branch railway line from Bohusevice to the fort, to the one man whose job it was to keep the clock mechanism in the closed Catholic church in order – this system had to be constantly supervised and statistically accounted for, particularly with respect to the total number of inmates of the ghetto, an uncommonly time-consuming business going far beyond civilian requirements when you remember that new transports were arriving all the time, and people were regularly weeded out to be sent elsewhere with their files marked *R.N.E.* for *Rückkehr Nicht Erwünscht*, Return Not Desired, a purpose for which the SS men responsible, who regarded numerical accuracy as one of their highest principles, had a census taken several times, on one occasion, if I remember correctly, said Austerlitz, on 10 November 1943 outside the gates in the open fields of the Bohusevice basin, when the entire population of the ghetto – children, old people and any of the sick at all able to walk not excepted – was marched out after assembling in the barracks yards at dawn to be drawn up in block formation behind numbered wooden boards, and there, throughout the whole of this cold and damp day, as the fog drifted over the fields, they were forced to wait, guarded by armed police and not permitted to step out of line even for a minute, for the SS men to arrive, as they eventually did on their motorbikes at three o'clock, to carry out the count of heads and then repeat it twice before they could feel convinced that the final result, including those few still within the walls, did in fact tally with the expected number of forty thousand one hundred and forty-five, whereupon they rode away again in some haste, entirely forgetting to give any orders for the inmates' return, so that this great crowd of many one of those perverse formulations, were adorned with pretty fairy-tale friezes and equipped with sand-pits, paddling pools and merry-go-rounds, whilst the former OREL cinema, which until now had served as a dumping ground for the oldest inmates of the ghetto and where a huge chandelier still hung from the ceiling in the dark space inside, was converted within a few weeks into a concert hall and theatre, and elsewhere shops stocked with goods from the SS storehouses were opened for the sale of food and household utensils, ladies' and gentlemen's clothing, shoes, underwear, travel requisites and suitcases; there were also a convalescent home, a chapel, a lending library, a gymnasium, a post office, a bank where the manager's office was furnished with a sort of field marshal's desk and a suite of easy chairs, not to mention a coffee-house with sun umbrellas and folding chairs outside it to suggest the agreeable atmosphere of a resort inviting all passers-by to linger for a while, and indeed there was no end to the improvements and embellishments, with much sawing, hammering and painting until the time of the visit itself approached and Theresienstadt, after another seven and a half thousand of the less presentable inmates had been sent east amidst all this busy activity, to thin out the population, so to speak, became a Potemkin village or sham Eldorado which may have dazzled even some of the inhabitants themselves and where, when the appointed day came, the commission of two Danes and one Swiss official, having been guided, in conformity with a precise plan and a timetable drawn up by the Kommandant's office, through the streets and over the spotless pavements, scrubbed with soap early that morning, could see for themselves the friendly, happy folk who had been spared the horrors of war and were looking out of the windows, could see how smartly they were all dressed, how well the few sick people were cared for, how they were given proper meals served on plates, how the bread ration was handed out by people in white drill gloves, how posters advertising sporting events, cabarets, theatrical performances and concerts were being put up on every corner and how, when the day's work was over, the residents of the town flocked out in their thousands on the ramparts and bastions to take the air, almost as if they were passengers enjoying an evening stroll on the deck of an ocean-going steamer, a most reassuring spectacle, all things considered, which the Germans, whether for propaganda purposes or in order to justify their actions and conduct to themselves, thought fit after the end of the Red Cross visit to record in a film, which Adler tells us, said Austerlitz, was given a soundtrack of Jewish folk music in March 1945, when a considerable number of the people who had appeared in it were no longer alive, and a copy of which, again according to Adler, had apparently turned up in the British-occupied zone after the war, although he, Adler himself, said Austerlitz, never saw it, and thought it was now lost without trace. For months, said Austerlitz, I tried in vain, through the good offices of the Imperial War Museum and other agencies, to find any clue to the present location of that film, since although I had been to Theresienstadt before leaving Prague, and despite Adler's meticulous account, which I had read down to the last footnote with the greatest attention, I found myself unable to cast my mind back to the ghetto and picture my mother Agáta there at the time. I kept thinking that if only the film could be found I might perhaps be able to see or gain some inkling of what it was really like, and then I imagined recognizing Agáta, beyond any possibility of doubt, a young woman as she would be by comparison with me today, perhaps among the guests outside the fake coffee-house, or a saleswoman in the haberdashery shop, just taking a fine pair of gloves carefully out of one of the drawers, or singing the part of Olympia in the *Tales of Hoffmann* which, so Adler says, was staged in Theresienstadt in the course of the improvements campaign. I imagined seeing her walking down the street in a summer dress and lightweight gabardine coat, said Austerlitz: among a group of ghetto residents out for a stroll, she alone seemed to make straight for me, coming closer with every step, until at last I thought I could sense her stepping out of the frame and passing over into me. It was wishful fantasies such as these which cast me into a state of great excitement when the Imperial War Museum finally succeeded, through the Federal Archives in Berlin, in obtaining a cassette copy of the film of Theresienstadt for which I had been searching. I remember very clearly, said Austerlitz, how I sat in one of the museum's video viewing rooms, placed the cassette in the black opening of the recorder with trembling hands, and then, although unable to take in any of it, watched various tasks being carried out at the anvil and forge of a smithy, in the pottery and wood-carving workshop, in the handbag-making and shoe-manufacturing sections –

images into my head; they merely flickered before my eyes as the source of continual irritation or vexation, which was further reinforced when, to my horror, it turned out that the Berlin cassette inscribed with the original title of *Der Führer schenkt den Juden eine Stadt* had on it only a patchwork of scenes cobbled together and lasting some fourteen minutes, scarcely more than an opening sequence in which, despite the hopes I had entertained, I could not see Agáta anywhere, however often I ran the tape and however hard I strained to make her out among those fleeting faces. In the end the impossibility of seeing anything more closely in those pictures, which seemed to dissolve even as they appeared, said Austerlitz, gave me the idea of having a slow-motion copy of this fragment from Theresienstadt made, one which would last a whole hour, and indeed once the scant document was extended to four times its original length, it did reveal previously hidden objects and people, creating, by default as it were, a different sort of film altogether, which I have since watched over and over again. The men and women employed in the workshops now looked as if they were toiling in their sleep, so long did it take them to draw needle and thread through the air as they

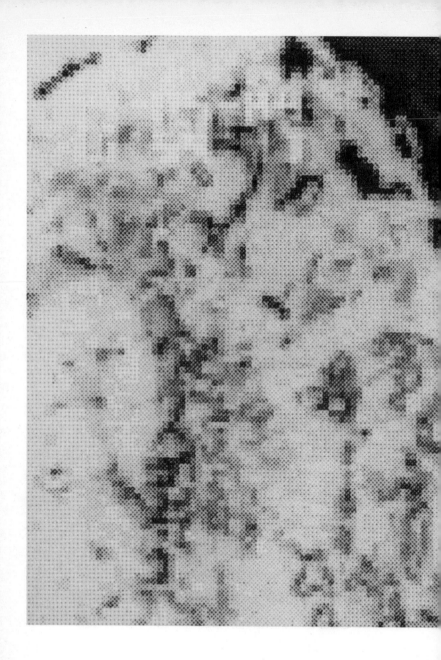

stitched, so heavily did their eyelids sink, so slowly did their lips move as they looked wearily up at the camera. They seemed to be hovering rather than walking, as if their feet no longer quite touched the ground. The contours of their bodies were blurred and, particularly in the scenes shot out of doors in broad daylight, had dissolved at the edges, resembling, as it occurred to me, said Austerlitz, the frayed outlines of the human hand shown in the fluidal pictures and electrographs taken by Louis Draget in Paris around the turn of the century. The many damaged sections of the tape, which I had hardly noticed before, now melted the image from its centre or from the edges, blotting it out and instead making patterns of bright white sprinkled with black which reminded me of aerial photographs taken in the far north, or a drop of water seen under the microscope. Strangest of all, however, said Austerlitz, was the transformation of sounds in this slow-motion version. In a brief sequence at the very beginning, showing red-hot iron being worked in a smithy to shoe a draught ox, the merry polka by some Austrian operetta composer on the soundtrack of the Berlin copy had become a funeral march dragging along at a grotesquely sluggish pace, and the rest of the musical pieces accompanying the film, among which I could identify only the can-can from *La Vie Parisienne* and the scherzo from Mendelssohn's *Midsummer Night's Dream*, also moved in a kind of subterranean world, through the most nightmarish depths, said Austerlitz, to which no human voice has ever descended. None of the words of the commentary could be distinguished any more. At the point where, on the original Berlin copy, a male voice, in high-pitched, strenuous tones forced through the larynx, had spoken of task forces and cohorts of workers deployed, as circumstances required, in various different ways, or if necessary retrained, so that everyone willing to work – *jeder Arbeitswillige!*, so Austerlitz interrupted himself – had an opportunity of fitting seamlessly into the production process, at this point of the tape all that could now be made out, Austerlitz continued, was a menacing growl such as I had heard only once before in my life, on an unseasonably hot May Day many years ago in the Jardin des Plantes in Paris when, after one of the peculiar turns that often came over me in those days, I rested for a while on a park bench beside an aviary not far from the big cats' house, where the lions and tigers, invisible from my vantage point and, as it struck me at the time, said Austerlitz, driven out of their minds in captivity, raised their hollow roars of lament hour after hour without ceasing. And then, Austerlitz continued, towards the end of the film there was the comparatively long sequence showing the first performance of a piece of music composed in Theresienstadt, Pavel Haas's study for string orchestra, if I am not mistaken. The series of frames begins with a view into the hall from the back. The windows are wide open, and a large audience is sitting not in rows as usual at a concert, but as if they were in some sort of tavern or hotel dining-room, in groups of four around tables. The chairs, probably made specially for the occasion in the carpentry workshop of the ghetto, are of pseudo-Tyrolean design with heart shapes sawn out of their backs. In the course of the performance the camera lingers in close-up over several members of the audience, including an old gentleman whose cropped grey head fills the right-hand side of the picture, while at the left-hand side, set a little way back and close to the upper edge of the frame, the face of a young woman appears, barely emerging from the black shadows around it, which is why I did not notice it at all at first. Around her neck, said Austerlitz, she is

wearing a three-stringed and delicately draped neck-lace which scarcely stands out from her dark, high-necked dress, and there is, I think, a white flower in her hair. She looks, so I tell myself as I watch, just as I imagined the singer Agáta from my faint memories and the few other clues to her appearance that I now have, and I gaze and gaze again at that face, which seems to me both strange and familiar, said Austerlitz, I run the tape back repeatedly, looking at the time indicator in the top left-hand corner of the screen, where the figures covering part of her fore-head show the minutes and seconds, from 10:53 to 10:57, while the hundredths of a second flash by so fast that you cannot read and capture them. — At

built as his summer residence by Archduke
Ferdinand of the Tyrol, which Vera had told me
was a favourite destination of Agáta and Maximilian on their excursions out of the city. I also
spent several days searching the records for the
years 1938 and 1939 in the Prague theatrical
archives in the Celetná, and there, among letters,
files on employees, programmes and faded newspaper cuttings, I came upon the photograph of an
anonymous actress who seemed to resemble my
dim memory of my mother, and in whom Vera,
who had already spent some time studying the face
of the woman in the concert audience which I had
copied from the Theresienstadt film, before shak-
ing her head and putting it aside, immediately and
without a shadow of doubt, as she said, recognized

Agáta as she had then been. — During this part of his tale, Austerlitz and I had walked from the cemetery behind St Clement's Hospital all the way back to Liverpool Street. When we took leave of each other outside the railway station, Auster-litz gave me an envelope which he had with him and which contained the photograph from the theatrical archives in Prague, as a memento, he said, for he told me that he was now about to go to Paris to search for traces of his father's last move-ments, and to transport himself back to the time when he too had lived there, in one way feeling liberated from the false pretences of his English life, but in another oppressed by the vague sense that he did not belong in this city either, or indeed anywhere else in the world.

*

It was in September of the same year that I received a postcard from Austerlitz giving me his new address (6 rue des cinq Diamants, in the thirteenth arrondissement), which I knew was in the nature of an invitation to visit him as soon as it could be arranged. When I arrived at the Gare du Nord, high summer temperatures still prevailed, at the of all who for any reason ventured out of doors, wearing masks to protect their faces. We both watched these calamitous images from the other end of the earth for some time before Austerlitz, as usual without any preamble, continued his story. When I was first in Paris at the end of the 1950s, he said, turning to me, I had a room in the apartment of an elderly lady of almost transparent appearance called Amélie Cerf, who lived at No. 6, rue Emile Zola, not far from the Pont Mirabeau, a shapeless concrete block which I still sometimes see in my nightmares today. On my return now I had really meant to find somewhere to stay in the same street, but then after all I decided to rent a place here in the thirteenth arrondissement, since my father, Maximilian Aychenwald, whose last known address was in the rue Barrault, must have frequented this area at least for a while before, as it seems, he disappeared irrevocably and without trace. At any rate, my inquiries at the house in the rue Barrault, most of which is now empty, were fruitless, and so were my inquiries at various agencies in the prefecture, partly because of the proverbially unhelpful attitude of Parisian officials, which was even more marked than usual on account of

the interminable hot summer weather, and partly because I myself found it increasingly difficult to go from one bureau to another making what I was coming to conclude were useless requests for further information. Soon I was merely wandering without any aim or plan in mind down the streets leading away from the boulevard Auguste Blanqui, up to the Place d'Italie on one side and back down to the Glacière on the other, always thinking, against all reason, that I might suddenly see my father appear out of nowhere, coming towards me or stepping out of an entrance. I sat in this bar too for hours on end, trying to imagine him in his plum-coloured double-breasted suit, perhaps a little threadbare now, bent over one of the café tables and writing those letters to his loved ones in Prague which never arrived. I kept wondering whether he had been interned in the half-built housing estate out at Drancy after the first police raid in Paris in August 1941, or not until July of the following year, when a whole army of French gendarmes took thirteen thousand of their Jewish fellow citizens from their homes, in what was called the *grande rafle*, during which over a hundred of their victims jumped out of the windows in events already existed and were only waiting for us to find our way to them at last, just as when we have accepted an invitation we duly arrive in a certain house at a given time. And might it not be, continued Austerlitz, that we also have appointments to keep in the past, in what has gone before and is for the most part extinguished, and must go there in search of places and people who have some connection with us on the far side of time, so to speak? For instance, one curiously gloomy morning recently I was in the Cimetière de Montparnasse, laid out by the Hospitallers in the seventeenth century on land belonging to the Hôtel de Dieu and now surrounded by towering office blocks, walking among the gravestones erected in a vaguely segregated part in memory of members of the Woelfflin, Wormser, Mayerbeer, Ginsberg, Franck and many other Jewish families, and I felt as if, despite knowing nothing of my origins for so long, I had lingered among them before, or as if they were still accompanying me. I read all their euphonious German names and retained them in my mind – thinking of my land-lady in the rue Emile Zola and of a certain Hippolyte Cerf who was born in Neuf Brisach in

1807, probably as Hippolyt Hirsch, and according to the inscription had died in Paris on the eighth of March 1890, the sixteenth of Adar 5650, many years after his marriage to one Antoinette Fulda of Frankfurt. Among the children of these forebears who had moved from Germany to the French capital were Adolphe and Alfonse, together with Jeanne and Pauline, who had brought Messrs Lanzberg and Ochs into the family as sons-in-law, and a generation later came Hugo and Lucie Sussfeld, née Ochs, who had a memorial plaque half hidden by a dried-up asparagus fern inside the cramped mausoleum, informing visitors to the grave that the couple had died on being deported in 1944. Since that time which, as I told myself while attempting to decipher, through the sparse stems of the asparagus fern, the letters forming the words *morts en déportation*, was now half a century ago, since that time, said Austerlitz, not much more than a dozen years had passed before I moved into Amélie Cerf's apartment in the rue Emile Zola with my few belongings. What, I wondered, are twelve or thirteen such years, if not a single moment of unalterable pain? Was Amélie Cerf, whom I remember as physically almost non-existent, perhaps the last surviving member of her tribe? Was there no one left to put up a memorial to her in the family mausoleum? Did she ever come to lie in that tomb at all, or did she dissolve into the empty air like Hugo and Lucie? As for myself, Austerlitz continued his story after a long pause, during my first stay in Paris, and indeed later in my life as well, I tried not to let anything distract me from my studies. In the week I went daily to the Bibliothèque Nationale in the rue Richelieu, and usually remained in my place there until evening, in silent solidarity with the many others immersed in their intellectual labours, losing myself in the small print of the footnotes to the works I was reading, in the books I found mentioned in those notes, then in the footnotes to those books in their own turn, and so escaping from factual, scholarly accounts to the strangest of details, in a kind of continual regression expressed in the form of my own marginal remarks and glosses, which increasingly diverged into the most varied and impenetrable of ramifications. My neighbour was usually an elderly gentleman with carefully trimmed hair and sleeve protectors, who had been working for decades on an encyclopaedia of church history, a project which had now reached the letter K, so that it was obvious he would never be able to complete it. Without the slightest hesitation, and never making any corrections, he filled in one after another of his index cards in tiny copperplate handwriting, subsequently setting them out in front of him in meticulous order. Some years later, said Auster-litz, when I was watching a short black and white film about the Bibliothèque Nationale and saw messages racing by pneumatic post from the reading-rooms to the stacks, along what might be described as the library's nervous system, it struck me that the scholars, together with the whole apparatus of the library, formed an immensely complex and constantly evolving creature which had to be fed with myriads of words, in order to bring forth myriads of words in its own turn. I think that this film, which I saw only once but which assumed ever more monstrous and fantastic dimensions in my imagination, was entitled *Toute la mémoire du monde* and was made by Alain Resnais. Even before then my mind often dwelt on the question of whether there in the reading-room of the library, which was full of a quiet humming, rustling and clearing of throats, I was on the Islands of the

Blest or, on the contrary, in a penal colony, and that conundrum, said Austerlitz, was going round in my head again on a day which has lodged itself with particular tenacity in my memory, a day when I spent perhaps as much as an hour in the manuscripts and records department on the first floor, where I was temporarily working, looking out at the tall rows of windows on the opposite side of the building, which reflected the dark slates of the roof, at the narrow brick-red chimneys, the bright and icy-blue sky, and the snow-white metal weather vane with the shape of a swallow cut out of it, soaring upwards and as blue as the azure of the sky itself. The reflections in the old glass panes were slightly irregular or undulating, and I remember, said Austerlitz, that at the sight of them, for some reason I could not understand, tears came to my eyes. It was on the same day, added Austerlitz, that Marie de Verneuil, who was working in the records department too and must have noticed my strange fit of melancholy, pushed a note over to me asking me to join her for a cup of coffee. In the state I was in at the time I did not stop to reflect on the unconventionality of her conduct, but nodded in silent acceptance of her invitation and went out

with her, almost obediently, one might say, said
Austerlitz, downstairs, across the inner courtyard
and through the library gates, down several of the
streets so full of pleasant air that fresh and somehow festive morning, and over to the Palais Royal,
where we sat for a long time under the arcades
beside a shop window in which, as I recollect, said
Austerlitz, hundreds and hundreds of tin soldiers in
the brightly coloured uniforms of the Napoleonic
army were drawn up in marching order and battle
formation. On that first encounter, and indeed
later, Marie told me very little about herself and
her background, perhaps because she came from a
very distinguished family, while as she probably
guessed I was from nowhere, so to speak. Once we
had discovered our common interests, our conversation in the café under the arcade, during which
Marie alternately ordered peppermint tea and
vanilla ice cream, turned mainly on subjects of
architectural history, including, as I still remember
very clearly, said Austerlitz, a paper-mill in the
Charente which Marie had visited with a cousin of
hers not long before and which by her account of it
was one of the strangest places she had ever seen.
This enormous building, made of oak beams and

sometimes groaning under its own weight, said Marie, stands half hidden among trees and bushes on the bend of a river with waters of a deep, almost unnatural green. Inside the mill two brothers, each proficient in his own skills, one of whom had a squint and the other a crooked shoulder, turn great masses of soaked paper and rags of fabric into clean sheets of blank paper, which are then dried on the racks of a large airing loft at the top of the mill. You are surrounded by a quiet twilight there, said Marie, you see the light of day outside through cracks in the slatted blinds, you hear water running gently over the weir, and the heavy turning of the mill wheel, and you wish for nothing more but eternal peace. Everything Marie meant to me from then on, said Austerlitz, was summed up in this tale of the paper-mill in which, without speaking of herself, she revealed her inner being to me. In the weeks and months that followed, Austerlitz continued, we often strolled together in the Jardin du Luxembourg, the Tuileries and the Jardin des Plantes, walking up and down the esplanade between the well-pruned plane trees with the west front of the Natural History Museum now on our right and now on our left, going into the palm

brèche d'incompréhension. Marie spent every second or third weekend, continued Austerlitz, his narrative taking another direction, with her parents or wider family, who owned several estates in the wooded country around Compiègne or further north in Picardy. At those times when she was not in Paris, which always cast me into an anxious mood, I regularly set off to explore the outlying districts of the city, taking the Métro out to Montreuil, Malakoff, Charenton, Bobigny, Bagnolet, Le Pré St Germain, St Denis, St Mandé or elsewhere, to walk through the empty Sunday streets taking hundreds of *banlieu*-photographs, as I called them, pictures which in their very emptiness, as I realized only later, reflected my orphaned frame of mind. It was on such a suburban expedition, one unusually oppressive Sunday in September when grey storm-clouds were rolling over the sky from the south-west, that I went out to Maisons-Alfort and there discovered the museum of veterinary medicine, of which I had never heard before, in the extensive grounds of the Ecole Vétérinaire, itself founded two hundred years ago. An old Moroccan sat at the entrance, wearing a kind of burnous, with a fez on his head. I still have the twenty-franc ticket he sold me in my wallet, said Austerlitz, and taking it out he handed it to me over the table of the bistro where we were

sitting as if there were something very special about it. Inside the museum, Austerlitz continued, I did not meet another living soul, either in the well-proportioned stairway or in the three exhibition rooms on the first floor. All the more uncanny in the ambient silence, which was merely emphasized by the creaking of the floorboards beneath my feet, seemed the exhibits assembled in the glass-fronted cases reaching almost to the ceiling, and dating without exception from the end of the eighteenth or the beginning of the nineteenth century. There were plaster casts of the jaws of many different kinds of ruminants and rodents; kidney stones which had been found in circus camels, as large and spherically perfect as skittle-balls; the cross-section of a piglet only a few hours old, its organs rendered transparent by a process of chemical diaphanization and now floating in the liquid around it like a deep-sea fish which would never see the light of day; the pale-blue foetus of a foal, where the quicksilver injected as a contrast medium into the network of veins beneath its thin skin had formed patterns like frost flowers as it leeched out; the skulls and skeletons of many different creatures; whole digestive systems in formaldehyde; pathologically malformed organs, shrunken hearts and bloated livers; trees of bronchial tubes, some of them three feet high, their petrified and rust-coloured branches looking

like coral growths; and in the teratological department there were monstrosities of every imaginable
and unimaginable kind, Janus-faced and two-
headed calves, Cyclopean beasts with outsized
foreheads, a human infant born in Maisons-Alfort
on the day when the Emperor was exiled to the
island of St Helena, its legs fused together so that
it resembled a mermaid, a ten-legged sheep, and
truly horrific creatures consisting of little more
than a scrap of skin, a crooked wing and half a claw.
Far the most awesome of all, however, so said
Austerlitz, was the exhibit in a glass case at the back
of the last cabinet of the museum, the life-sized
figure of a horseman, very skilfully flayed in the
post-Revolutionary period by the anatomist and
dissector Honoré Fragonard, who was then at the
height of his fame, so that every strand in the
tensed muscles of the rider and his mount, which
was racing forward with a panic-stricken expression, was clearly visible in the colours of congealed
blood, together with the blue of the veins and
the ochre yellow of the sinews and ligaments.
Fragonard, who was descended from the famous
family of Provençal perfumiers, said Austerlitz,
had apparently dissected over three thousand

afternoon heat as I left the museum, I recollected that as I walked along beside the wall I felt that I had reached steep and impassable terrain, and that I had wanted to sit down but none the less walked on, into the bright rays of the sun, until I came to the Métro station where I had to wait endlessly, as it seemed to me, in the brooding darkness of the tunnel for the next train to come in. The carriage in which I travelled towards the Bastille, said Austerlitz, was not very full. Later I remembered a gypsy playing the accordion, and a very dark Indo-Chinese woman with an alarmingly thin face and eyes sunk deep in their sockets. Of the few other passengers, I could recollect only that they were all looking out of the side windows of the train into the darkness, where there was nothing to be seen but a pallid reflection of the carriage where they sat. Gradually I also came to remember suddenly feeling unwell during the journey, with a phantom pain spreading through my chest, and thinking I was about to die of the weak heart I have inherited, from whom I do not know. I did not return to my senses until I was in the Salpêtrière, to which I had been taken and where I was now lying in one of the men's wards, containing perhaps forty patients at last I began to improve, said Austerlitz, I also recollected how once, while my mind was still quite submerged, I had seen myself standing, filled with a painful sense that something within me was trying to surface from oblivion, in front of a poster painted in bold brushstrokes which was pasted to the tunnel wall and showed a happy family on a winter holiday in Chamonix. The peaks of the mountains towered snow white in the background, with a wonderful blue sky above them, the straight upper edge of which did not entirely hide a yellowed notice issued by the Paris city council in July 1943. Who knows, said Austerlitz, what would have become of me there in the Salpêtrière – when I could remember nothing about myself, or my own previous history, or anything else whatsoever, and as I was told later I kept babbling disconnectedly in various languages – who knows what would have become of me had it not been for one of the nursing staff, a man with fiery red hair and flickering eyes called Quentin Quignard, who looked in my notebook and under the barely legible initials M. de V. found the address 7, place des Vosges, written by Marie in a blank space among my notes after our first conversation at the café in lious mop of hair and green eyes the colour of iced water who stumbled over the hem of her raincoat, which was much too long for her, as she was playing with her skipping rope in one of the lime-white squares in the Luxembourg gardens and grazed her right knee, a scene regarded by Marie as a *déjà vu* because, she said, over twenty years ago just the same accident had happened to her at exactly the same place, an incident which at the time seemed to her shameful and aroused in her the first premonitions of death. Not long afterwards, one Saturday afternoon when a cold mist hung low in the air, we wandered through the half-deserted area between the tracks of the Gare d'Austerlitz and the Quai d'Austerlitz on the left bank of the Seine, slowly finding our way among abandoned dockyards, boarded-up warehouses, goods depots, customs halls and a few garages and car-repair shops. In one of the empty spaces not far from the station itself, the Bastiani Travelling Circus had erected its small tent, much mended and wreathed in strings of orange electric lights. By tacit agreement, we entered just as the performance was coming to a close. A few dozen women and children were seated on low stools round the ring – not that it was really a ring, said Austerlitz, rather it was a vague sort of rondelle on which a few shovelfuls of sawdust had been thrown, so hemmed in by the front row of spectators that even a pony could hardly have trotted round it in a circle. We were just in time for the last number, featuring a conjuror in a dark-blue cloak who produced from his top hat a bantam cockerel with wonderfully coloured plumage, not much bigger than a magpie or a raven. This brightly hued bird, obviously completely tame, went over a kind of miniature show-jumping course consisting of all manner of little steps, ladders and other obstacles which he had to negotiate, gave the right answer to sums such as two times three or four minus one by clattering his beak when the conjurer showed him cards with the figures written on them, at a whispered command lay down on the ground to fall asleep, resting in a curious position on his side with his wings outspread, and finally disappeared into the top hat again. After the conjuror's exit the lights slowly dimmed, and when our eyes were used to the darkness we saw a quantity of stars traced in luminous paint inside the top of the tent, giving the impression that we were really out of doors.

somewhere very distant, from the East, I thought, from the Caucasus or Turkey. Nor can I say what was suggested to my mind by the sounds produced by the players, none of whom, I am sure, could read musical notation. Sometimes I seemed to hear a long-forgotten Welsh hymn in their melodies, or then again, very softly yet making the senses swirl, the revolutions of a waltz, a ländler theme, or the slow sound of a funeral march, which put me in mind of the curiously halting progress of a uniformed guard of honour escorting a body to its last resting place, and of how, in their ceremonious manner, they pause every time before taking the next step, with one foot suspended an inch above the ground for the briefest of moments. I still do not understand, said Austerlitz, what was happening within me as I listened to this extraordinarily foreign nocturnal music conjured out of thin air, so to speak, by the circus performers with their slightly out-of-tune instruments, nor could I have said at the time whether my heart was contracting in pain or expanding with happiness for the first time in my life. Why certain tonal colours, subtleties of key and syncopations can take such a hold on the mind is something that an entirely

unmusical person like myself can never understand, said Austerlitz, but today, looking back, it
seems to me as if the mystery which touched me at
the time was summed up in the image of the snow-
white goose standing motionless and steadfast
among the musicians as long as they played. Neck
craning forward slightly, pale eyelids slightly
lowered, it listened there in the tent beneath
that shimmering firmament of painted stars
until the last notes had died away, as if it knew its
own future and the fate of its present companions.
— As I might perhaps be aware, said Austerlitz,
taking up his tale again at our next meeting at

the Brasserie Le Havane, the new Bibliothèque Nationale bearing the name of the French President now stands on what over the years had become the increasingly dilapidated area on the left bank of the Seine, where he and Marie de Verneuil had once attended that unforgettable circus performance. The old library in the rue Richelieu has been closed, as I saw for myself not long ago, said Austerlitz, the domed hall with its green porcelain lampshades which cast such a soothing, pleasant light is deserted, the books have been taken off the shelves, and the readers, who once sat at the desks numbered with little enamel

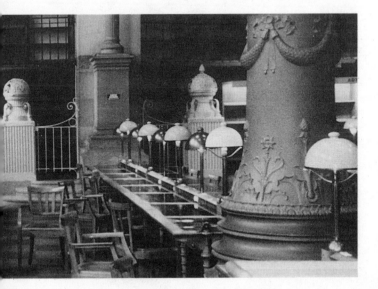

plates, in close contact with their neighbours and silent harmony with those who had gone before them, might have vanished from the face of the earth. I do not think, said Austerlitz, that many of the old readers go out to the new library on the Quai François Mauriac. In order to reach the Grande Bibliothèque you have to travel through a desolate no-man's-land in one of those robot-driven Métro trains steered by a ghostly voice, or alternatively you have to catch a bus in the Place Valhubert and then walk along the windswept river bank towards the hideous, outsize building, the monumental dimensions of which were evidently inspired by the late President's wish to perpetuate his memory whilst, perhaps because it had to serve this purpose, it was so conceived that it is, as I realized on my first visit, said Austerlitz, both in its outer appearance and inner constitution unwelcoming if not inimical to human beings, and runs counter, on principle, one might say, to the requirements of any true reader. If you approach the new Bibliothèque Nationale from the Place Valhubert you find yourself at the foot of a flight of steps which, made out of countless grooved hardwood boards and measuring three hundred by a hundred and fifty metres, surrounds the entire complex on the two sides facing the street like the lower storey of a ziggurat. Once you have climbed the steps, at least four dozen in number and as closely set as they are steep, a venture not entirely without its dangers even for younger visitors, said Austerlitz, you are standing on an esplanade which positively overwhelms the eye, built of the same grooved wood as the steps, and extending over an area about the size of nine football pitches between the four corner towers of the library which thrust their way twenty-two floors up into the air. You might think, especially on days when the wind drives rain over this totally exposed platform, as it quite often does, said Austerlitz, that by some mistake you had found your way to the deck of the *Berengaria* or one of the other ocean-going giants, and you would be not in the least surprised if, to the sound of a wailing foghorn, the horizon of the city of Paris suddenly began rising and falling against the gauge of the towers as the great steamer pounded onwards through mountainous waves, or if one of the tiny figures, having unwisely ventured on deck, were swept over the rail by a gust of wind and carried far out into the

upholstered benches and small chairs like folding stools where visitors to the library can perch only in such a way that their knees are almost level with their heads, so that my first thought at the sight of them, said Austerlitz, was that the people whom I saw crouching so close to the ground, some by themselves and some in small groups, were members of a wandering tribe encamped here on their way through the Sahara or the Sinai desert in the last glow of the setting sun, in order to await the coming of darkness. And of course, Austerlitz continued, you cannot leave the red Sinai hall for the inner citadel of the library without more ado; first you have to put your request at an information point staffed by half a dozen ladies, whereupon, if this request to any degree exceeds the very simplest contingency, you take a number, like a visitor to a tax office; you then have to wait, often for half an hour or more, until another member of staff calls you into a separate cubicle, as if you were on business of an extremely dubious nature, or at least had to be dealt with away from the public gaze, and here you must say again what it is you have come for and receive the relevant instructions. Despite such measures of control I finally ends of their balancing poles quivering, or as if, always on the edge of invisibility, I saw dodging now here, now there, those two mythical squirrels said to have been brought to the library in the hope that they will increase and multiply, founding a large colony of their species in this artificial pine grove to entertain any readers who look up from their books now and then. And several times, said Austerlitz, birds which had lost their way in the library forest flew into the mirror images of the trees in the reading-room windows, struck the glass with a dull thud, and fell lifeless to the ground. Sitting at my place in the reading-room, said Austerlitz, I thought at length about the way in which such unforeseen accidents, the fall of a single creature to its death when diverted from its natural path, or the recurrent symptoms of paralysis affecting the electronic data retrieval system, relate to the Cartesian overall plan of the Bibliothèque Nationale, and I came to the conclusion that in any project we design and develop, the size and degree of complexity of the information and control systems inscribed in it are the crucial factors, so that the all-embracing and absolute perfection of the concept can in practice coincide, the ground. Years later, after long wanderings across Germany, the colonel, risen from the dead, so to speak, returns to Paris to claim his rights to his estates, to his wife the Comtesse Ferraud who has now remarried, and to his own name. He is presented as a ghostly figure, said Austerlitz, standing in the lawyer Derville's office, a gaunt and desiccated old soldier, as we are told at this point. His eyes appear half-blind, veiled as they are by a mother-of-pearl gleam, flickering unsteadily like candle flames. His face is pale, its lines sharp as a knife edge. Around his neck he wears a shabby cravat of black silk. *Je suis le Colonel Chabert, celui qui est mort à Eylau* are the words with which he introduces himself, and then he tells the tale of the mass grave (a *fosse des morts*, as Balzac describes it, said Austerlitz), into which he was thrown the day after the battle along with the rest of the fallen, and where he finally came to himself, as he says, in excruciating pain. *J'entendis, ou crus entendre*, Austerlitz quoted from memory, looking out of the brasserie window at the boulevard August Blanqui, *des gémissements poussés par le monde des cadavres au milieu duquel je gisais. Et quoique la mémoire de ces moments soit bien ténébreuse, quoique mes souvenirs soient bien confus, malgré les impressions de souffrances encore plus profondes que je devais éprouver et qui ont brouillé mes idées, il y a des nuits où je crois encore entendre ces soupirs étouffés.* Only a few days after reading this book, the more melodramatic aspects of which, Austerlitz continued, reinforced the suspicion I had always entertained that the border between life and death is less impermeable than we commonly think, I was in the reading-room again and, on opening an American architectural journal – this was at exactly six in the evening – I came upon a large-format photograph showing the room filled with open shelves up to the ceiling where the files on the prisoners in the little fortress of Terezín, as it is called, are kept today. I remembered, said Austerlitz, that at the time of my first visit to the Bohemian ghetto I could not bring myself to enter the outworks on the glacis to the south of the star-shaped town, and perhaps that was why, at the sight of the records room, a kind of *idée fixe* forced itself upon me that, all along, my true place of work should have been there in the little fortress of Terezín, where so many had perished in the cold, damp casemates, and it was my own fault that I had not taken it up.

As I was tormenting myself with such thoughts, distinctly aware, so Austerlitz continued, that my face was being marked by the signs of that anguish which so often assails me, I was approached by one of the library staff called Henri Lemoine, who had recognized me from those early years of mine in Paris when I went daily to the rue Richelieu. Jacques Austerlitz, inquired Lemoine, stopping by my desk and leaning slightly down to me, and so, said Austerlitz, we began a long, whispered conversation in the *Haut-de-jardin* reading-room, which was gradually emptying now, about the dissolution, in line with the inexorable spread of processed data, of our capacity to remember, and about the collapse, *l'effondrement*, as Lemoine put it, of the Bibliothèque Nationale which is already underway. The new library building, which in both its entire layout and its near-ludicrous internal regulation seeks to exclude the reader as a potential enemy, might be described, so Lemoine thought, said Austerlitz, as the official manifestation of the increasingly importunate urge to break with everything which still has some living connection to the past. At a certain point in our conversation, said Austerlitz, and in response to a casual request of mine, Lemoine took me up to the eighteenth floor of the south-east tower, where one can look down from the so-called belvedere at the entire urban agglomeration which has risen over the millennia from the land beneath its foundations, which is now entirely hollowed out: a pale limestone range, a kind of excrescence extending the concentric spread of its incrustations far beyond the boulevards Davout, Soult, Poniatowski, Masséna and Kellermann, and on into the outermost periphery beyond the suburbs, which now lay in the haze of twilight. A few miles to the south-east there was a faint green mark in the even grey, with a kind of blunt cone rising from it which Lemoine identified as the monkeys' hill in the Bois de Vincennes. Closer to hand, we saw the convoluted traffic routes on which trains and cars crawled back and forth like black beetles and caterpillars. It was strange, said Lemoine, but up here he always had the impression that life moved silently and slowly down below, that the body of the city had been infected by an obscure disease spreading underground, and I remembered, said Austerlitz, when Lemoine made this remark, the winter months of the year 1959 during which I was studying the

haps, he added, that is only a reflex of the aware-
ness formed in my mind over the years of the various layers which have been superimposed on each
other to form the carapace of the city. Thus, on the
waste land between the marshalling yard of the
Gare d'Austerlitz and the Pont Tolbiac where this
Babylonian library now rises, there stood until the
end of the war an extensive warehousing complex
to which the Germans brought all the loot they had
taken from the homes of the Jews of Paris. I believe
they cleared some forty thousand apartments at
that time, said Lemoine, in an operation lasting
months, for which purpose they requisitioned the
entire pantechnicon fleet of the Paris Union of
Furniture Removers, and an army of no fewer than
fifteen hundred removal men was brought into
action. All who had taken part in any way in this
highly organized programme of expropriation and
reutilization, said Lemoine, the people in charge of
it, the sometimes rival staffs of the occupying
power and the financial and fiscal authorities, the
residents' and property registries, the banks and
insurance agencies, the police, the transport firms,
the landlords and caretakers of the apartment
buildings, must undoubtedly have known that

forth. More than seven hundred train-loads left from here for the ruined cities of the Reich. Not infrequently, said Lemoine, Party grandees on visits from Germany and high-ranking SS and Wehrmacht officers stationed in Paris would walk around the halls of the depot, known to the prisoners as Les Galéries d'Austerlitz, with their wives or other ladies, choosing drawing-room furniture for a Grunewald villa, or a Sèvres dinner service, a fur coat or a Pleyel piano. The most valuable items, of course, were not sent off wholesale to the bombed cities, and no one will now admit to knowing where they went, for the fact is that the whole affair is buried in the most literal sense beneath the foundations of our pharaonic President's Grande Bibliothèque, said Lemoine. The last of the light faded away down on the empty promenades. The tree-tops of the pine grove, which from this high vantage point had resembled moss-covered ground, now formed a regular black rectangle. For a while, said Austerlitz, we stood together in silence on the library belvedere, looking out over the city where it lay now sparkling in the light of its lamps.

*

When I met Austerlitz again for morning coffee on the boulevard Auguste Blanqui, shortly before I left Paris, he told me that the previous day he had heard, from one of the staff at the records centre in the rue Geoffroy-l'Asnier, that Maximilian Aychenwald had been interned during the latter part of 1942 in the camp at Gurs, a place in the Pyrenean foothills which he, Austerlitz, must now seek out. Curiously enough, said Austerlitz, a few hours after our last meeting, when he had come back from the Bibliothèque Nationale and changed

trains at the Gare d'Austerlitz, he had felt a premonition that he was coming closer to his father. As I might know, he said, part of the railway network had been paralysed by a strike last Wednesday, and in the unusual silence which, as a consequence, had descended on the Gare d'Austerlitz, an idea came to him of his father's leaving Paris from this station, close as it was to his flat in the rue Barrault, soon after the Germans entered the city. I imagined, said Austerlitz, that I saw him leaning out of the window of his

compartment as the train left, and I saw the white clouds of smoke rising from the locomotive as it began to move ponderously away. After that I wandered round the deserted station half dazed, through the labyrinthine underpasses, over footbridges, up flights of steps on one side and down on the other. That station, said Austerlitz, has always seemed to me the most mysterious of all the railway terminals of Paris. I spent many hours in it during my student days, and even wrote a kind of memorandum on its layout and history. At the time I was particularly fascinated by the way the Métro trains coming from the Bastille, having crossed the Seine, roll over the iron viaduct into the station's upper storey, quite as if the façade were swallowing them up. And I also remember that I felt an uneasiness induced by the hall behind this façade, filled with a feeble light and almost entirely empty, where, on a platform roughly assembled out of beams and boards, there stood a scaffolding reminiscent of a gallows with all kinds of rusty iron hooks, which I was told later was used as a bicycle store. When I first set foot on this platform years ago, on a Sunday afternoon in the middle of the vacation period, however, there was not a bicycle to be seen, and perhaps for that reason, or perhaps because of the plucked pigeon feathers lying all over the floorboards, an impression forced itself upon me of being on the scene of some unexpiated crime. What is more, said Austerlitz, that sinister wooden structure still exists. Even the grey pigeon feathers have not yet blown away. And there are dark patches, of leaked axle grease, perhaps, or carbolineum, or something altogether different, one can't tell. Moreover, I was disturbed by the fact that, as I stood on the scaffolding that Sunday afternoon looking up through the dim light at the ornate ironwork of the north façade, two tiny figures which I had noticed only after some time were moving about

on ropes, carrying out repair work, like black spiders in their web. — I don't know, said Austerlitz, what all this means, and so I am going to continue looking for my father, and for Marie de Verneuil as well. It was nearly twelve o'clock when we took leave of each other outside the Glacière Métro station. Years ago, Austerlitz said as we parted, there were great swamps here where people skated in winter, just as they did outside Bishopsgate in London, and then he gave me the key to his house in Alderney Street. I could stay there whenever I liked, he said, and study the black and white photographs which, one day, would be all that was left of his life. And I should not omit, he added, to ring the bell at the gateway in the brick wall adjoining his house, for behind that wall, although he had never been able to see it from any of his windows, there was a plot where lime trees and lilacs grew and in which members of the Ashkenazi community had been buried ever since the eighteenth century, including Rabbi David Tevele Schiff and Rabbi Samuel Falk, the Baal Shem of London. He had discovered the cemetery, from which, as he now suspected, the moths used to fly into his house, said Austerlitz,

only a few days before he left London, when the
gate in the wall stood open for the first time in all
the years he had lived in Alderney Street. Inside, a
very small, almost dwarf-like woman of perhaps
seventy years old — the cemetery caretaker, as it
turned out — was walking along the paths between
the graves in her slippers. Beside her, almost as

tall as she was, walked a Belgian sheepdog now
grey with age who answered to the name of Billie
and was very timid. In the bright spring light shining through the newly opened leaves of the lime
trees you might have thought, Austerlitz told me,
that you had entered a fairy tale which, like life
itself, had grown older with the passing of time. I
for my part could not get the story of the cemetery in Alderney Street with which Austerlitz had

taken his leave of me out of my head, and that may have been why I stopped in Antwerp on my way back from Paris, to see the Nocturama again and go out to Breendonk once more. I spent a disturbed night in a hotel on the Astridsplein, in an ugly room with brown wallpaper looking out on fire-walls, ventilation chimneys and flat roofs separated from each other by barbed wire at the

back of the building. I think there was some kind of popular festival going on in the city at the time; in any case, the wailing of ambulance and police sirens went on until early in the morning. When at last I woke from a bad dream I saw the tiny silver arrows of aeroplanes passing at intervals of ten or twelve minutes through the bright-blue space above the neighbouring houses, which still lay in twilight. On leaving the Flamingo Hotel −

such was its name, if I remember correctly – at about eight o'clock, I saw a pale-faced woman of about forty with her eyes turned away lying on a high trolley down by the reception desk, where there was no one in evidence. Two ambulance men were talking out on the pavement. I crossed the Astridsplein to the station, bought myself a coffee, and took the next suburban train to Mechelen, then walking the ten remaining kilometres to Willebroek through the suburbs and the now built-up outskirts of the town. I retained hardly anything of what I saw on my way. All I remember is a peculiarly narrow house, in fact no more than one room wide, built of puce-coloured brick and standing in an equally narrow strip of garden surrounded by a tall thuya hedge. A canal ran beside this house, and a long barge laden with cabbages as big and round as cannonballs was gliding along it just as I passed, apparently without any boatman to steer it and leaving not a trace on the black surface of the water. It had turned unusually hot, just as it was thirty years ago, by the time I reached Willebroek. The fortifications lay unchanged on the blue-green island, but the number of visitors had increased. There were several coaches in the car park, while inside the porter's lodge a troop of schoolchildren in brightly coloured clothes was crowding around the cash desk and the small kiosk. Some of them had already gone ahead of the rest over the bridge to the dark gate through which, yet again, I could not bring myself to pass even after long hesitation. I spent some time in one of the hut-like wooden buildings where the SS had set up a printing shop for the manufacture of various official forms and greetings cards. The roof and the walls creaked in the heat, and the thought passed through my mind that the hair on my head might catch fire, as St Julian's did on his way through the desert. Later I sat beside the moat surrounding the fortress. In the distance, beyond the penal colony, the fence and the watch towers, I saw the high-rise blocks of Mechelen encroaching further and further on the fields and the countryside. A grey goose was swimming on the dark water, going a little way in one direction and then a little way back in the other. After a while it scrambled up on the bank and settled on the grass not far from me. I took the book Austerlitz had given me on our first meeting in Paris out of my rucksack. It was by Dan Jacobson (a colleague of his, although unknown to him all these years, Austerlitz had said), and it described the author's search for his grandfather Rabbi Yisrael Yehoshua Melamed, known as Heshel. All that had come down from Heshel to his grandson was a pocket calendar, his Russian identity papers, a worn spectacle case containing not only his glasses but a faded and already disintegrating piece of silk, and a studio photograph of Heshel in a black coat with a black velour top hat on his head. His one eye, or so at least it looks on the cover of the book, is shaded; in the other it is just possible to make out a white fleck, the light of life extinguished when Heshel died of a heart attack at the age of fifty-three soon after the First World War. It was this premature death which made Menuchah, the rabbi's wife, decide in 1920 to emigrate with her nine children from Lithuania to South Africa, and that was also the reason why Jacobson himself spent most of his childhood in the town of Kimberley, near the diamond mines of the same name. Most of the mines, so I read as I sat there opposite the fortifications of Breendonk, were already disused at the time, including the two largest, the Kimberley and De Beers mines, and since they were not fenced off anyone who liked could venture to the edge of those vast pits and look down to a depth of several thousand feet. Jacobson writes that it was truly terrifying to see such emptiness open up a foot away from firm ground, to realize that there was no transition, only this dividing line, with ordinary life on one side and its unimaginable opposite on the other. The chasm into which no ray of light could penetrate was Jacobson's image of the vanished past of his family and his people which, as he knows, can never be brought up from those depths again. On his travels in Lithuania Jacobson finds scarcely any trace of his forebears, only signs everywhere of the annihilation from which Heshel's weak heart had preserved his immediate family when it stopped beating. Of the town of Kaunas, where Heshel had his photograph taken all those years ago, Jacobson tells us that the Russians built a ring of twelve fortresses around it in the late nineteenth century, which then in 1914, despite the elevated positions on which they had been constructed, and for all the great number of their cannon, the thickness of their walls and their labyrinthine corridors, proved entirely useless.

Some of the forts, writes Jacobson, fell into disrepair later, others served the Lithuanians and then the Russians once more as prisons. In 1941 they fell into German hands, including the notorious Fort IX where Wehrmacht command posts were set up and where more than thirty thousand people were killed over the next three years. Their remains, says Jacobson, lie under a field of oats a hundred metres outside the walls. Transports from the west kept coming to Kaunas until May 1944, when the war had long since been lost, as the last messages from those locked in the dungeons of the fortress bear witness. One of them, writes Jacobson, scratched the words *Nous sommes neuf cents Français* on the cold limestone wall of the bunker. Others left only a date and place of origin with their names: Lob, Marcel, de St. Nazaire; Wechsler, Abram, de Limoges; Max Stern, Paris, 18.5.44. Sitting by the moat of the fortress of Breendonk, I read to the end of the fifteenth chapter of *Heshel's Kingdom*, and then set out on my way back to Mechelen, reaching the town as evening began to fall.